KOLKATA NOIR

TOM VATER

PRAISE FOR TOM VATER

"There's a tremendous – and tremendously fresh – energy to Tom Vater's writing."

"The narrative is fast-paced and the frequent action scenes are convincingly written. The smells and sounds of Cambodia are vividly brought to life. Maier is a bold and brave hero."

"This is noir at its grittiest, most graphic best. There is a lush complexity in the narrative that Mr. Vater has brought us readers. To say this was a historically laden story is to sell it short. We are transported into the world of Cambodia, and quite possibly one that most of us will never see in real life. The magic, the awe, the mystique and mystery all accompany the depth of characterization."

"The Cambodian Book of the Dead is an enigmatic, unsettling thriller that never lets you get your balance."

"Exuberant writing."

OTHER BOOKS BY TOM VATER

The Devil's Road to Kathmandu

The Cambodian Book of the Dead (Detective Maier Mystery, Book 1)
The Man with the Golden Mind (Detective Maier Mystery, Book 2)
The Monsoon Ghost Image (Detective Maier Mystery, Book 3)

Sacred Skin (with Aroon Thaewchatturat)
Burmese Light (with Hans Kemp)
Cambodia: Journey through the Land of the Khmer (with Kraig Lieb)

PREFACE

In 2019, I was selected as artist in residence for the annual Indo-European Art Residency Kolkata by the Goethe-Institut/Max Mueller Bhavan. I wrote the first draft of Kolkata Noir at 77 Sarat Bose Road in Ballygunge.

I'm deeply grateful to have had the opportunity to explore and reflect on Kolkata for two months, a tough, fascinating, complicated, often contradictory city with a huge personality, wonderful people, incredible architecture and public spaces and a vibrant art scene.

To the people of Kolkata

PART ONE

1999 – CALCUTTA

PAULAMI ROYCHOWDHURY LOVED THE VIEW. Richard was lying on the unmade bed, his smooth, tanned chest rising and falling in silence. Beyond the prone figure of the boy, she could see the Oberoi Hotel's swimming pool, surrounded by polished tropical foliage, reflecting the late morning Calcutta sun. Waiters in white, starched livery moved silently between bathers, dispensing cocktails, mocktails, and other refreshments best added up in dollars. Life. Somewhere far away she could hear the roar of the city. For a moment Paulami wished the image would freeze, suspended in time and space, her eyes forever fixed on the inert, perfect shape on the bed, afloat in one of the city's most salubrious private hotel suites.

She caught her reflection in the oversized mirror. Getting older was a drag. Abir, who spent his nights in filthy Chinatown music bars, ogling women ten times more tired than herself, was good for nothing but his money. The irony of having to spend so much of his money to get away from him wasn't lost on her. Having to hide a little scandalous behavior from the neighbors in Bagh Bazaar, while he came home drunk, was like a sore she'd been scratching for years. Annoyed, she kicked one of the legs of the four-poster, scuffing her gold-embroidered Punjabi juttis on the dark wood.

She would have loved to stay with this boy, the first white boy she'd been with since returning from her studies in Leeds twenty years earlier. Richard had managed to pry her from her gilded cage. But the longing would pass. Richard wouldn't be able to solve her problems. Still, one could always use a thorn to remove a thorn.

The air-conditioning was turned up too high. Shivering into her best Baluchuri sari, Paulami snapped out of her well-deserved revelry. Her gaze drifted away from the movie scene she'd created for herself. She let go and sashayed away from her lover towards the phone. Things to do, people to call. Life in Calcutta wasn't a holiday. Life in Calcutta was murder. And time was its most reliable assassin.

———

The lift operator, a small, grizzled man from UP who hadn't seen the sun in years, showed Madhurima Mitra into the bar. She'd never set foot in the Broadway Hotel. She certainly had never been in the hotel's ground floor night spot, now virtually empty and smelling of stale cigarette smoke, spilt beer, and the kind of existences she had little time for outside her professional life. Madhurima didn't go to bars. At least the air-conditioning worked.

It was easy to spot Becker, the only foreigner in the dingy room, installed at a small table, a large bottle of Kingfisher in front of him. Who drank at 6pm? She thanked the lift man and wound her way between the tightly packed tables towards Becker. She'd checked the hotel register. He was a photographer. He'd booked in for a week.

As she got closer, she made a quick appraisal. She already knew Becker was in his mid-20s, a few years younger than herself. He had provided an address in London and had entered the country on a six-month tourist visa, also issued in London. The hotel had furnished her with a C form and a photostat of his passport. The foreigner was sitting down, but she could tell that he was pretty tall. Broad shoulders, a face a little too worn for his age, ash blonde hair. His tan confirmed that he'd been in India for a month. His eyes. She looked away as he returned her gaze.

"Good afternoon. Are you Mr. Becker?"

Becker smiled. Madhurima was the kind of woman who always smiled back, at the appropriate frequency. Everyone deserved a smile. Those who didn't got one anyway. A smile was professional. It was defense. It was authority. The foreigner smiled a little more and made an inviting gesture towards the worn chintz chair across his table. She stood. It gave her more self-confidence. It was proper, she supposed, as proper as her smile. She was on duty. And even if she hadn't been... But then she wouldn't be here. She'd be at the gym, at home, somewhere. Not at the Broadway, not drinking beer.

"I'm Inspectress Madhurima Mitra, Kolkata Police. Nice to meet you, Mr. Becker."

Becker stood up. He was a little slow doing so. Definitely not in a hurry. He held out his hand, probably to make up for his reticence. His touch was cool and light as a feather. Madhurima suspected that his handshake varied as much as his smile. She had to admit that hers did too. The moment was a little awkward, a little too long, but quite acceptable in the bar's dim, rusty, old movie light.

"What am I supposed to have done, Ms. Mitra?" his voice trailed off. She detected a hint of concern on his face. Deep down everyone was guilty of something.

"You've done nothing we might be concerned about..." she trailed off for a little dramatic effect. "Not at this moment, anyhow. I'm investigating the disappearance of Richard Dunlop, a British citizen. He rents a room in this hotel."

Becker relaxed.

"Could you step out to the reception, please, Mr. Becker?"

3

"If you want the entire hotel staff and half of Ganesh Chandra Avenue to discuss our conversation for the next couple of days, then that's the best option."

She was annoyed for a second. He was right. And he was rude. But she moved on, pulled out the chair he'd offered her, and sat. He wasn't the first rude man she'd encountered. A waiter came past with the drinks' menu. She waved him away before he'd reached the table.

"When did you last see Mr. Dunlop?"

"Four days ago, in almost exactly the same seat you're sitting in now."

She opened a notepad and pulled a biro from her breast pocket.

"What time was that?"

"Closing time. We had four beers and he told me his life story."

She jotted down everything he said. First impressions were important.

"He's been found dead?"

She shook her head. The foreigner could sense there was something she wasn't telling him.

"I appreciate your cooperation, Mr. Becker. We have no reason to believe that Mr. Dunlop is dead. But he's been missing for four days."

"If something happened to Richard, I'd be glad to help."

"You are a photographer?"

Becker nodded, more to himself than to her.

"I'm sure you know that already."

"You don't like the police?"

Becker pulled himself upright.

"I'm sorry if I gave you that impression. I am here to help."

"Can you tell me more about him?"

"He's a bit weird. He has almost no money. He's been all over, Jaisalmer, Goa, Hampi. Too many tourists, he told me, so he came east. Richard told me he liked Calcutta, he described the city in quite lyrical terms — he mentioned the morning fog on the Hooghly, the crumbling Raj buildings, the food. He talked about Bengali women."

Becker looked at her with an expression she couldn't quite read before he continued.

"He told me he bagged a degree in German from Leeds a few months ago and was trying to put as many miles between his academic past and his current self as possible. He was trying to find something, but he wasn't sure what. Adventure and glory, he said. At one point, quite a few beers into an evening, he shouted 'Independence or death'. He was definitely driven, restless."

"So, you felt sorry for him."

Becker didn't look like he minded sitting in bars alone. He almost looked part of the furniture.

"He was the only other foreigner drinking down here every night. He didn't strike me as the kind of guy who goes nuts because he's been in India too long. Perhaps he isn't lost at all, just broke and in need of a beer while planning his next move. Now I think about it, what he told me about his life in the UK was more revealing than what he told me about what he'd been up to in India. He hated being in Leeds. Perhaps something traumatic happened to him there. He was a man on the run, so to speak."

Madhurima raised her eyebrows.

Becker corrected himself, "I didn't mean that in the sense of Richard being a criminal fugitive. If he was, you'd know by now, I guess."

"What did he say about Bengali women?"

Becker shifted in his seat, looking like a man who'd already said too much. As if information he'd furnish on Richard Dunlop might sound like a reflection on himself. She felt oddly touched by the thought.

"He told me Bengali women were beautiful. He said this could be a place where a young man might fall in love. At the time, I didn't think much about it, and I didn't press him. He's right, of course."

He was looking directly at her. There was nothing leery in his expression, but Madhurima blushed anyway. She noted his answer on her pad, hoping the dim light in the bar was on her side.

"Did you have the impression he was…" she was looking for the right words, "he had met a woman here?"

"Yes, I did, but as I said, I didn't ask any questions. He didn't volunteer anything else."

Madhurima relaxed. The foreigner was helpful. More helpful than her colleagues back at the Bowbazar Station, who'd saddled her with the case of the missing tourist because no one was keen to investigate the whereabouts of foreigners. And because they wanted her to fail. All except Emran. He was on her side. The others didn't want to see a woman rise through the ranks. One day they might have to take orders from her.

"So, he ran off with a rich woman?"

His question made her uncomfortable. He was giving her goosebumps. She wasn't entirely sure how much to tell him. He wasn't supposed to be asking questions. That was her job.

"It's possible."

Becker shrugged and took a sip of beer and waved for a second bottle.

"If you tell me what really happened, I can perhaps make some suggestions. I know Richard a little. He was gregarious and very private at the same time."

"He would run off with an older woman?"

Becker laughed. Short and dry. "Well, I guess he did, if you put it like this."

"You didn't answer my question."

"You're not telling me what happened."

She searched his face, though she didn't exactly know what for. She realized that she held back not just because he was a witness in an investigation that might have far-reaching, career-defining consequences, but because he was a foreigner. But she might need a foreigner to find a foreigner. She tried to look Becker in the eyes, but there was something else there from which she recoiled. If she were really honest to herself, it was her, not him, that bothered her. His calm, friendly demeanor, his apparent helpfulness, his non-judgmental gaze, and the subtle negation of it that floated in the way he looked at her, flustered her. Madhurima pulled herself together and came to a decision.

"Richard Dunlop checked into the Oberoi, the finest hotel in the city, with a local woman called Paulami Roychowdhury four days ago. Did he tell you about her?"

Becker shook his head.

"I guess they've checked out since, destination unknown?"

"Yes, destination unknown. That's a nice way of putting it."

He smiled. She blushed again. She wasn't used to working with foreigners, she decided. But her great uncle, her role model, Calcutta's most celebrated detective in the 1960s, had always told her: when in doubt, take a leap. Especially a leap of inquiry. He'd told her again and again that her mind was the most powerful weapon at her disposal. That's how she'd gotten to where she was today. Another leap wouldn't hurt.

"Mr. Becker, I need more than this. Mrs. Roychowdhury is a well-known, wealthy, socialite from North Kolkata. She's old money. Her elopement will scandalize the entire city. I need to find her. And Mr. Dunlop, of course. Not just for his sake, but for mine too."

Becker raised a questioning eyebrow. She envied him his calm.

"I was assigned this case because it's a social disaster. Her husband is old Calcutta money. Her brother-in-law owns one of the finest properties in North Calcutta. If I fail to find Mrs. Roychowdhury and Mr. Dunlop both alive and well, I'll be pushed into traffic duty."

The door to reception creaked open. A uniformed cop stuck his head inside the bar. He waved for her with some urgency.

She couldn't very well ignore him, but she took her time wrapping up her interview. Looking flustered in front of her subordinates, or for that matter, the foreigner, wasn't an option. She got up with economic ease, not a gesture of uncertainty in her movements that might have betrayed her insecurity. Becker was just too damn calm.

"We will meet again. Please don't leave the city. In fact, please stay in the hotel this evening. I may have to get back to you soon."

"I'll be right here talking to my little, brown friends."

She was incensed, then she realized he was talking about his bottles of Kingfisher. There was so much room for misunderstandings with outsiders. That added an extra challenge to her situation. But she had to admit to herself, it wasn't all bad. Becker was interesting. He was cooperating. And she liked his eyes, even as she couldn't really hold his gaze. Nor could she explain exactly why that might be the case. There was something loose about the way he looked at her. Perhaps some things didn't need to be understood quite as properly as she generally expected.

Outside in the real world, a car was waiting for her at the crowded curb. Assistant Commissioner Mazumdar sat in the back. He looked impatient. Madhurima wouldn't have been at all surprised to find out that he was friends with the Roychowdhurys. He was cut from the same cloth. And he was here because something had happened. Something terrible.

———

Paulami hadn't been to Kishore's rajbari, her husband's family's stately home in Shobha Bazaar, for years. Abir had told her in drunken bouts of sentimentality about growing up beneath Belgian chandeliers, surrounded by vases from China and oil paintings of Indian landscapes by long forgotten Britishers. When the brothers had inherited the sprawling building, they'd immediately fallen out over money. While Abir enjoyed a stellar career as one of the city's top transport engineers, Kishore had invested whatever funds had been handed down by the family into transforming part of the mansion into a hotel. But for all its fading zamindar glory and Kishore's unique art collection, the building's location, in the heart of what had once been called Black Town (as opposed to White Town where the Britishers had lived, further south), had kept the tourists away. When the hotel had opened its doors, offering twelve huge rooms crammed with antiques, the newspapers had rightly pointed out that the property stood on the edge of Sonagachi, Calcutta's most notorious red-light area. A trickle of foreign tourists, unaware of the less than salubrious surroundings, continued to check in, but the domestic travelers stayed away. The rot, Abir had told Paulami, had soon set in again.

Nonetheless, Roychowdhury Mansion was impressive. A dispirited-looking guard waved Paulami and Richard through the heavy, wrought-iron gate onto a gravel drive. A marble fountain topped by a swan, long defunct, sat in the middle of an uneven lawn. The main building loomed a hundred regal meters ahead, a two-story architectural mélange of Bengali and Raj aesthetics, fronted by a classical colonnade and a broad stairway that rose from an unruly lawn. Paulami had no desire to live in the place. She imagined it would be draughty and wasn't heated in winter, but she couldn't help be impressed by 170 years' worth of urban splendor. She'd married into the right family. Just not to the right man.

Richard didn't hide his astonishment. He stared at the building, transfixed, then turned towards Paulami. He was almost manic with joy, as if he'd found something that he'd been looking for a long time.

"That's incredible. What an amazing building. I feel so...privileged to have met you," he said turning his attention back to the building.

"Come, meet my brother-in-law Kishore."

They crossed the lawn and started up the steps. At the top of the steps, Richard looked back at the garden slope towards the fence that ran along the far end of the property, and was lined with neem trees. She imagined him as a young prince, surveying his realm, though there was something discomfiting in the thought, despite its sensuous subtext.

Paulami's brother-in-law wrenched her out of her reverie. He was a good-looking man, trim, and straight-backed, his raven-black hair greased back, a little younger than her husband, a lot less wracked by alcohol, and altogether more presentable. She felt like a maharani, flanked by her two lovers. But today, Kishore didn't shine, so she felt disconcerted a second time, by a second man.

"Paulami, sister, you're mad coming here. The whole city's looking for you. They have a young and ambitious female inspector on your case. I just saw the news on Doordarshan."

"What are you talking about, Kishore? Is Abir behind this? Why does this city care if I abscond with my friend Richard for a couple of nights? Is this where we are at as a society? I was at the damn Oberoi only. I paid my taxes for this year. Well, Abir did."

Kishore didn't laugh, didn't even smile at her quip. His eyes flicked from her to Richard and back.

"Abir is dead."

The news hit her like a fist. Of course, it wasn't news. It was the plan. But if she hadn't known better, she might have thought Kishore was genuinely distressed. He put on a great show for Richard. He was totally in character. She felt sick. Abir was dead. Finally. It was utterly shocking. She'd only seen him very much alive, if inebriated, three nights ago.

"The cops are coming here to interview me. If they find you here and they find you guilty, I will be an accessory to your crime. It's monstrous."

"How did they say he died?"

Kishore wiped a thick film of sweat from his forehead. He

seemed to struggle telling her. In fact, her brother-in-law looked utterly confused. He deserved an Oscar.

"He was bludgeoned to death in a back alley in Bowbazar. Stuffed into a crate, they only found him this afternoon. The murder weapon has been traced to that den of iniquity, the Broadway Hotel, some kind of heavy tool they use to fix their lift. Abir had been in the box for three days. Thousands passed him, while he lay there dead."

Something felt wrong. Paulami had only spoken to Kishore the previous day from her suite at the Oberoi. He'd let nothing slip about the fact that the deed had been done. She guessed he was being careful not to implicate himself on the phone. But still.

Richard gazed wistfully at the lawn while they talked. He was more tourist than prince now. Out of his depth. Or zoned out. And she was a murder suspect. Paulami Roychowdhury, you are a murder suspect, she intoned silently. It was monstrous. She'd have to fix that.

"You must go. Leave the city. Take the car. Don't take the train. If you go to the police, you're done. Both of you. They'll convict you, if only because of your scandalous behavior. And whoever murdered my brother will go scot-free."

Richard, his head lowered, descended a few steps. Paulami tried to sense where she was at. Was he disgusted? Was he in shock? Did he still love her, like he'd told her so many times? What did that mean now? Would their plan come together? It was time to go. Without another word to Kishore, she followed the young man.

———

Becker stood in the Mission Café, burning through his second coffee. Madhurima watched him from the pavement. He looked untroubled. He snapped a couple of pictures. He joked around with the staff. All around her, the city was waking up. Men, women, and children crowded around a fire hydrant that spewed water into the gutter, washing themselves, lathering themselves in thick layers of soap; the women dressed in shalwar kameez, the men with gamchas around their waists, the children naked and screaming. The mornings were innocent. The day's struggles hadn't ground the street people down yet. There was joy and optimism in the mornings. Today would be better than yesterday, and tomorrow would be better than today. She admired her fellow Calcuttans for their faith. Faith would still be there tomorrow. Better governance probably wouldn't. Becker spotted her and waved. She went inside.

"Coffee."

She nodded. This wasn't going to be easy.

"Good morning, Mr. Becker."

He smiled depreciatively.

"Just call me Becker."

She tried to smile back, visibly untrammeled by emotional baggage, she hoped.

"Fine, please call me Madhu."

"I guess you wouldn't be back first thing in the morning, if there wasn't some news. Has Richard turned up?"

"Have you watched TV?"

He shook his head.

"Never even switched it on yet. I don't speak Bengali. What's the deal? You left pretty quickly last night."

"Sorry, I didn't mean to be impolite. My boss was outside, with bad news."

He raised his eyebrows questioningly. It made him look less severe.

"We don't know where Paulami Roychowdhury and Richard Dunlop are. We have combed the city's better hotels. There's been a terrible development."

Becker said nothing. She was grateful he didn't feel the need to second guess her. He just stood waiting.

"Mrs. Roychowdhury's husband was found dead late yesterday. Across the road from here, around the corner from the Broadway."

Becker sucked in his breath. He quite obviously hadn't expected this.

"You think Richard did it for her? A crime of passion?"

"We'd like to ask him that. I think they have left town. I don't see where else they could be. We've asked all the relatives, acquaintances. No one's seen her. Except perhaps her brother-in-law. When we interviewed him, he seemed obviously distressed, but I felt something else. He might not have been telling me the whole truth. I mean, he was in mourning, but he was preoccupied at the same time."

"Thanks for sharing this with me. Am I a suspect?"

"No, of course not. Not in my book, anyway. But my boss wants me to explore all lines of inquiry. And the Calcutta police force would much rather arrest two foreigners who have collaborated on a murder than start apprehend members of our establishment."

"How did the husband die?"

"He was beaten about the head with an iron rod. A spare part for the elevator in the Broadway, it turns out."

"Yesterday?"

She shook her head.

"No, whoever killed him, hid him in a crate. He was probably killed three or four days ago."

"Perhaps that's before Richard disappeared. Could have been around the time I was hanging around with him."

She nodded and pulled her notepad from her breast pocket. She showed him a timeline she'd made.

"Yes, I am afraid that in theory that makes you a suspect too. And Mr. Roychowdhury's death was really rather violent. There was real force in the beating he received. We don't think his wife did it. Her lover might have had a motive and the means though."

"What does that have to do with me?"

"You admitted spending time with Richard on the day of the murder or just before. You're the only one who knew him. That makes you a person of interest."

Becker laughed, a bitter tone in his voice.

"That's why I love cops so much."

"I took the liberty to take your passport from the receptionist at the Broadway."

Becker sucked in his breath. "Am I under arrest?"

Madhurima knew she needed to tread very carefully now.

"Not at all. And I myself don't suspect you. Not at all. But my superiors want me to throw a very wide net. There is pressure from higher up to resolve this case. And some of my superiors don't believe I can do it."

"You seem capable."

"No need to flatter me, Becker. But yes, I know what I'm doing, and if I can crack this case, I will be in a lot of people's good books."

Becker grinned with something she chose to interpret as reassurance.

"What happens now? I have to report to the local police station every day?"

She shook her head.

"I need your help, Becker. I have half the station against me, the other half indifferent. I told you, my great uncle was a famous detective. Everyone in the city knows him. That's why I was interviewed by the press yesterday. People expect me to nab the culprits or to fail spectacularly. Mostly the latter. And you are our only link to the young man who eloped with a prime murder suspect."

Becker said nothing. He just looked at her, perhaps trying to decide whether he could trust her. Then he pulled a compact camera from his pocket and snapped her portrait.

"I tell you what. I'm sure they've gone to Puri, the seaside town. Richard mentioned it several times and was keen to go back. Really keen. If you go down there, take me with you. I've been before. If they're there, I'd like to speak to Richard first before your colleagues arrest and torture him."

She ignored his foreign outburst of bad taste. Law enforcement was what it was. But there was no call to judge her. Madhurima was proud to be cop, and she was determined to bring Abir Roychowdhury's killer to justice.

"Great. We will go. I will get train tickets. I know Puri quite well. My family used to go there on holidays, visit the temple and eat macha ghanta."

"What's that?"

"Fried fish head curry. You will love it, Becker. And we will catch ourselves a killer. But now I will go to see Kishore Roychowdhury, the victim's brother. He lives in the old family rajbari, one of the old Bengali homes in Calcutta. He tried to make a hotel out of it. Abir was an engineer, very successful, but a drunk. These two often clashed, sometimes very publicly."

———

Kishore was waiting for Madhurima on the stairs of his mansion. She'd lived in Calcutta all her life, had been in and out of the houses of wealthy zamindars, the old landowner elite, countless times, but still, she was impressed by the grandeur.

"You have an amazing home, Mr. Roychowdhury. It's one of the finest buildings I've seen in Calcutta."

Kishore looked nervous. Madhurima guessed him to be in his late 40s. He was lean and reasonably handsome. He also looked like a man in mourning. No doubt, his brother's death had punched the wind out of him. He led her into the palace's central courtyard. Two floors of galleries with countless doors leading off into countless rooms ran in a rectangle above their heads. The courtyard was open to the sky, though a netting had been fitted to keep the birds out. They sat at a low marble table on narrow benches that looked stylish but proved to be uncomfortable.

"I'm sorry to disturb you at this terrible time. I'm here to talk to you about…"

Kishore cut her off. "You are Feluda's grandniece, no?"

Madhurima nodded.

"If you're only a tenth as good as your great uncle, you will surely crack this case, Madam, no?"

"We're following various leads."

"Whatever happened to the man?"

"He retired some years back. He's an astrologer and sits in his house in Ballygunge buried in charts and horoscopes."

Kishore wasn't really listening. He was more of an observer than a listener. He couldn't stop appraising her in the most obvious manner, as if he were continually updating his chances of personal success if push came to shove. Madhurima wasn't sure how to interpret this. Did he doubt her competence, or was he hiding something? Or was he stupid enough to be making a pass at her?

"You have honed in on any suspects yet?"

She didn't answer. The man was out of sorts, exasperated. Of course, he was in mourning, but there was something else. And sometimes not answering a question led to revelations disguised as new questions.

"Why are you working with a foreigner? I heard that on TV. It's very unusual. What can he do?"

"Mr. Becker knew the British man your sister-in-law spent three nights at the Oberoi with."

She didn't expect him to slow down. And he didn't.

"Then perhaps he is the culprit. He had a motive if Paulami really eloped with him, as the press has been screaming on their front pages these last few days. It would be a perfect solution to this murder mystery…" he trailed off, looking at her, appraising her. "Perhaps my brother's killing is all down to a foreign plot to divide us."

"Perfect solutions are rare, Mr. Roychowdhury."

She watched him swallow. Something had finally slowed Kishore down. That same something was in the back of her mind, telling her to push the boat out a little further.

"I'll find out who killed your brother. The city is in shock and needs answers. You and your family need answers, and you are right to demand those. The Kolkata police is here to help you. We Care. We Dare."

He relaxed a little and managed a crooked smile.

"But where could they have run off to?"

As she got up and headed for the stairway, she turned his question over in her mind? Usually one didn't inform grieving relatives of progress in a murder investigation and Kishore's questions had been too plentiful and too pointed for her taste. She decided to take a risk.

"Your sister-in-law may have eloped to Puri to see Lord Jagannath. I promise we will explore all avenues of investigation."

Kishore's face lit up. Madhurima started down the stairs without another word.

"We'll be in touch."

When she turned, her host had already hurried back inside the building.

———

Howrah Station, India's oldest railway complex, was teeming with passengers, railway employees, and a cast of thousands of homeless souls — platform children, teenage glue sniffers, and sex workers eked out a living between the railway tracks. The homeless slept on the ground in front of passengers waiting for trains. But it wasn't all bad. Most people had somewhere to go. Almost 20 000 trains crisscrossed the subcontinent every day. More than a million people had found employment with the railways. There was method to the madness.

Madhurima loved the station. She was proud of what her country could achieve in the face of sheer insurmountable challenges. And in her childhood, her parents had often taken her south to Puri on the very same train she was to take today.

The overnight Howrah Puri Express was packed, but Madhurima had tapped into the tatkal tickets, which were issued on the day of departure, and managed to get two 2nd class sleeper tickets.

Becker had installed himself on the lower bench and ordered two chai. She sat down next to him, scanning the multitudes outside the carriage. Too many of them were squeezing into their carriage, loaded with huge pieces of luggage, children, and tiffin boxes.

"Nice you got the tickets at such short notice. The quicker we get down there the better."

She took this as a compliment. "We have a term for this — jugaad. It means we find creative ways to work around a problem. We manage to come up with solutions even when we lack the very resources to overcome our problems."

Becker laughed, "I wish we had such a mechanism back in England."

"You guys are so wealthy you can choose to do things by the book. We try to, but we can't always afford it. It's a major dilemma in the police force."

"I think we have significant structural problems doing things properly back home. Our big businesses pretend to act within the law, but = they operate just like the East India Company used to. But we prefer to keep that very much out of view. Expensive suits and meetings with politicians in the media, environmental vandalism and war in the streets or exported to other parts of the world. So, you guys naturally think it's greener on the other side. But challenge the capitalist hegemony in the West and you'll get to the limits of democracy and pluralism pretty quickly."

She laughed. "You obviously thought about that."

"It's what I photograph," he continued, making no concessions to her irony, "I make a living shooting both sides. A great American singer summed it up very simply."

Becker turned to her and started singing, quietly enough not to draw a crowd from their fellow passengers.

"I bet there's rich folks eatin'
In a fancy dinin' car..."

She was impressed. He had a good voice even if the tune was a little simple and lacked subtlety. She thought of her own role models and education.

"Our great poet Rabindranth Tagore, who won your prestigious Nobel prize, once commented on the zamindars, our landowner class who grew rich by collaborating with the Britishers exploiting our country, 'I know zamindars are like the leeches of the land, a parasite that feeds on living things.'"

"People like the Roychowdhurys?"

"Oh, Becker, like my great uncle, you have great magajastra. You see and you understand. Your brain is like a weapon."

He laughed and flagged down another tea seller who was squeezing through the crowded carriage.

"You keep mentioning this guy. Perhaps you could take me to meet him when this is finished."

She smiled back at him, cautiously. "That depends on the outcome of my investigation. Everything hinges on that. It will make or break me. It will enable me to face great uncle with pride. Or it'll make me hide in shame in a back office pulling ledgers for the rest of my life. The stakes couldn't be higher for me, Becker."

The tea seller handed her a clay cup. The train's whistle pierced the cacophony generated by thousands of passengers, and the Howrah Puri Express slowly lurched out of the station and into the tropical night.

———

Madhurima couldn't sleep. The carriage was air-conditioned and glacial. The incessant snoring of fellow passengers assaulted her from all directions. Somewhere further down the aisle, a child was playing with a Chinese-made plastic toy, a wheel grinding on a wheel, in endless short spasms that had neither rhythm nor grace. She felt like arresting the parents. Becker lay fast asleep below her. He slept silently, his face relaxed, a tiny smile playing around his lips. She quietly climbed down into the carriage corridor and headed for the nearest toilets. As soon as she opened the carriage door, the usual smell of urine and bidis assaulted her. The two cubicles at the end of the carriage were both locked. She decided to wait it out rather than trace her way back along the entire carriage to the next set of toilets when she picked up another smell: opium. It was unmistakable, the cold smell of the poppy. She knew it from her childhood; her family's chowkidar, an old man long dead had sometimes indulged. In fact, she'd kind of liked the narcotic's scent when she was a child. Someone was getting high in one of the restrooms. The carriage managers slept in a tiny bunk-bed cabin when off duty and the one behind her was empty. She quickly slipped inside and pulled the curtains. From her vantage point she could watch both toilet doors. If the staff came by, she had her ID to wave them away. She didn't have to wait long. The door to her right opened. Kishore stepped into the corridor, his eyes bloodshot and remote. He turned and stumbled off into the next carriage — also second class but no air-conditioning. So, he had followed them. He had walked right into her trap. She slipped quickly into the toilet Kishore had emerged from before returning to her bunk. The poppy's aroma followed her into her deep sleep.

———

Becker had two teas ready at first light. Madhurima folded her bunk up and they sat side-by-side looking at the new day rising through the carriage's grimy windows. Puri was a small, coastal city in Orissa, 300 miles to the south of Kolkata. Home to the famous Jagannath temple and long stretches of beach facing the Bay of Bengal, it was also the location of the Rath Yatra, one of her country's most spectacular festivals. Once a year, giant wooden chariots, pulled along the town's main thoroughfare by thousands of devotees, transported the temple's three deities to their summer holiday residence. Two weeks later, the same process played out in reverse. The start of the festival was just a few days away.

There was no sign of this in the verdant countryside they rode through. Miles of rice paddy in a thousand shades of green interspersed by palm trees and small village hamlets revealed themselves in the grey dawn. Children, driving their water buffaloes to pasture, waved at the passing train. Men and women were doing their ablutions by the tracks. It was as pastoral as in her childhood memories.

"What will we do when we get there? Bengalis travel there in their thousands, and there are countless hotels. Searching for Mrs. Roychowdhury in those will be impossible, and I don't want to alert the local constabulary unless absolutely necessary."

Becker grinned. "I know where to go. The foreigners all stay to the north of town on C.T Road. And Richard told me about a hotel he loved; the Z... The last one on the beach apparently. Some kind of mansion belonging to a local politician. If they're in town, they might have booked into this place. It sounds like it will be acceptable to Mrs. Roychowdhury."

"I saw Kishore last night."

"In your dreams?" Becker laughed.

"No, coming out of one of the carriage toilets after indulging in opium."

Becker raised his eyebrows. "So, the bait you threw into the conversation yesterday worked. You had a great hunch. Do you think he killed his brother and tried to implicate Richard by using the tool from the Broadway?"

"I wouldn't dare to speculate. We don't have enough information. It could just be that he's worried for his sister-in-law and doesn't trust the police to find her."

"We will find her."

His hand brushed against her shoulder and she recoiled a little, though not because she felt he was too close. In public, someone was always watching and judging, even 300 miles from home.

———

The Z Hotel was a handsome mansion set back from the main road in well-kept gardens, protected by a high wall and a tall gate.

Paulami Roychowdhury was pacing the hotel's back terrace. The roar of the waves breaking on the beach and the crows fighting in the garden's casuarinas were lost on her. Richard had been angry. It had been a real shock. She'd never seen him angry. She had no idea her gentle, young soul could get this angry. After she'd told him that she couldn't go to England with him in the foreseeable future, he'd first been crestfallen, but then he'd huffed and puffed and finally walked out. She wasn't sure why she had told him. It hardly mattered. Once the cops found her, she would confess all. That had been the plan. Never change the plan, her mantra had been ever since. Never change the plan, because if one did, all hell might break loose.

They'd found her.

"Good afternoon. I'm Inspectress Madhurima Mitra, Kolkata Police. You're Paulami Roychowdhury. Your husband was murdered four days ago in Bowbazar. I'm investigating your husband's murder. Would you care to tell me why are in Puri?"

The police woman was young and self-confident, but she already had that knowing and suspicious look that all police had. Behind her a foreigner loomed in the doorway to the terrace. She felt her pulse quicken. This wasn't going to be easy. She said nothing, merely nodded affirmatively, and slumped into one of the heavy wooden chairs lined up against a long table that stretched along the terrace.

"Mrs. Roychowdhury, this is Mr. Becker. He stayed next door to Richard Dunlop at the Broadway before Mr. Dunlop checked into the Oberoi with you on the day your husband was murdered."

Paulami straightened up and tried to look imperious. But the policewoman didn't seem to notice and continued, "We have reason to believe...

Paulami interrupted. "I didn't do it. I have nothing to do with my husband's death. I am completely shocked. I have an alibi. I was at the Oberoi on the day of the killing. I wasn't anywhere near the scene of the crime. You're right, I was with Richard. The Oberoi is one the few places in the city where one can enjoy privacy."

The policewoman looked non-plussed. She'd pulled a notepad from her trouser pocket. The foreigner just stood in the doorway, watching them.

"I didn't do it."

The policewoman smiled sympathetically.

"Did you and your husband have any problems in the time leading up to his murder? Did you have an argument?"

Paulami huffed as if the question was beneath her, before answering. "I don't have to justify myself. My alibi is solid. But as you've made your inquiries you will know that our marriage was...difficult. My husband drank and disappeared for days on end. It wasn't a happy marriage. But I didn't kill him, and I don't know who did. It's monstrous."

"But you're a free woman now, expecting a large inheritance."

With as much anger as she could muster, Paulami shot back. "It's hardly the time to talk about this now. Yes, I will inherit what's due to me. But I didn't kill him. Quite the contrary, I encouraged him many times to stop drinking and come home to his old life, our life. But he refused."

The police officer shook her head, "I am sorry, Madam, but it's very much the time to talk about it now. You will never have an audience as sympathetic as me. My male colleagues will pin this murder on you, whether there's rhyme and reason. They're waiting in the wings of Bowbazar for you. You'll do yourself a favor talking to me. And being frank of course."

Paulami looked at her again. She was good. She was professional. Appealing to her empathy wouldn't work. It was time to get the knives out.

"I am taking so much tension at present. I didn't follow the press. It was my brother-in-law who informed me of my husband's death. Only yesterday."

"You saw Kishore yesterday? At what time?"

"About ten in the morning. Richard was with me. He can confirm this."

The police woman said nothing, but Paulami could sense that there was something wrong. Would her story hold up? It bloody had to. Never ever change a story one has agreed on.

"Was Mr. Dunlop with you the entire time at the Oberoi? You never left the property?"

Paulami put her heart and soul into her next statement.

"Well, we checked in together, four days ago now, in the morning, around 10am. I didn't have an easy night, so I fell asleep in the afternoon. Richard went swimming. He was back in the evening, and we had dinner together. Room service. You can check."

"Where is Mr. Dunlop now?

Paulami shrugged. "I am not sure. He went down to the beach only. We had an argument earlier. I mean, this is so stressful. My husband is dead. He was beaten viciously, Kishore told me. I knew the police would track me down here. I will travel back to Kolkata and give whatever statements."

She so wanted these people to leave her alone. She'd done nothing. Nothing could be proven. They would find a way to unravel the mystery. In her favor. That was just the way things had always been for her.

She slumped back into her chair. The audience was over as far she was concerned. The performance had worn her out. She was all spent. The inspectress appeared to have no more questions and neither had the foreigner who hadn't said a word.

"I've taken your ID and Richard's passport. We will come to collect you later. I will see if we can fly back to Kolkata. Please don't leave the hotel. If Richard returns, be sure to tell him he must stay."

Paulami nodded across the terrace. Now she could hear the ocean beyond the hotel's high walls. The waves crashed with savage irregularity onto the beach. There was no stopping them. Every time another breaker rolled in, she sensed losing a little more time.

"Just one more question," the police woman added. "Do you love him? Or is this just a fling as a result of an unhappy marriage?"

Paulami tried to look irritated. "That's a very personal question, Miss…?"

"It's Mitra. And murder is often a very personal business."

"Yes, I do really like him. He is a great deal more pleasant than my late husband. That sounds callous. But you should have been there, day in and day out."

———

They left via the back door onto a narrow lane that led down to the beach.

"How are we going to find Richard?"

Becker smiled at her. He looked handsome in the midday sun. She found his silence reassuring. He let her do her job. He didn't butt in.

25

"I have an idea where he is. There's a hippy guest house on the beach. Most of the western budget travelers stay there. He told me about that place as well. It's where he would be if he hadn't shacked up with Madam. We can try, it's only a couple of minutes away."

"Do you think Mrs. Roychowdhury was telling the truth?"

He shrugged. "I guess some of it was true. But there was definitely a performance element. I had the feeling she knew you were coming. That someone was coming. And that she'd rehearsed what she told us. And yet, it all sounded plausible."

"Do you think she's safe?"

"Her husband's been murdered. Her brother-in-law and her lover are both in Puri. I guess either one could have done it. She didn't do it, I'm sure of that. She isn't the sort of woman who goes into a back alley and bashes her husband's brain in with an iron tool. I don't see her doing that. But I'm not sure she's not in on the murder in some other way. So yes, she could be in danger. She could also be dangerous."

"Exactly. Wasn't she betraying Richard when she told us he'd left for a swim? Why would she have mentioned that? I thought that very odd."

Madhurima was pleased with Becker's summary. She would return to the Z. to keep an eye on Mrs. Roychowdhury as soon as possible. They walked down to the beach. New hotels were sprouting up among a handful of colonial-era buildings, dwarfing the older structures. Soon the entire beach front would be plastered with new properties. It looked a little haphazard. Becker led her to a squat, old building that rested in a large garden compound facing the sea. The breeze carried a salty taste. The sign outside the property read Pink House. The building's color didn't disappoint.

They saw Richard as soon as they walked through the gate. He sat by himself in a small, wooden, grass-roofed pavilion, nursing a lime soda, entranced by the waves.

"Hi, Richard."

The young man snapped out of his daydreams. His expression was grim. He nodded to Becker, barely surprised, and briefly looked at Madhurima. She didn't care for what she saw in his eyes. They weren't like Becker's.

"Hi, Becker, mate. Wow. What's up? How'd you find me? And why are you here?"

"This is Inspectress Mitra, Kolkata Police. She would like to ask you a few questions. After Mrs. Roychowdhury's husband was killed, she's a bit concerned for her welfare. And I was a bit worried when you disappeared from the Broadway."

"To be honest, mate, I think I'm in a bit over my head. I mean, we did do a runner together, me and Paulami. But I never thought her husband would get killed. If anything, I was scared he was going to follow us or call the police on us. What a mess. I got nothing to do with this. I mean, I thought she might get some problems, things being as they are here. But I would have looked out for her. She's great."

"Mr. Dunlop, you were with Mrs. Roychowdhury the entire time at the Oberoi?"

"Well, yeah. Three days of luxury. Eating, drinking, swimming, and, you know, being together."

Madhurima didn't know what to make of the young man.

"Did you go swimming on the day you checked in?"

Richard laughed. "I went swimming every day I was there. Have you seen the pool? It's bloody amazing. Not another pool like this in the country. Clean, proper size, cocktails before you can even snap your fingers. It's amazing."

"Do you think Paulami likes you?"

Richard rolled his eyes. "Weird question, that. Of course she likes me. Would you take a foreigner you'd just met to a super luxe hotel for four days if you didn't like him? I mean we talked about going to the UK together. Paulami's marriage was a disaster. She was really unhappy," he caught himself then, "but that doesn't mean she killed her husband. And anyway, we were at the Oberoi when that happened. Maybe you should talk to her brother-in-law. Now he's a real piece of work. He's after her money, make no mistake."

"Have you met Kishore Roychowdhury?"

Richard took a sip of his drink and nodded. "Went to his house. Except it isn't a house, it's a blimmin' palace. Amazing."

"When did you visit the Roychowdhury residence?"

Richard looked at her carefully. "Yesterday morning. It didn't go well for Paulami, so we left quickly. It was him who told us about the murder. We had no idea. Didn't switch the telly on at the Oberoi," he smirked.

Madhurima ignored his suggestive comment. She hated men saying these kinds of things.

"How did Mr. Roychowdhury seem to you?"

"Well. He wasn't quite right in the head. Called Paulami a murder suspect. Told her to get out of town. I thought Puri was the best getaway. Give her time to think, what to do next. Because there's no way Paulami should go to jail."

"Did she tell him you were coming down here?"

Richard looked away before answering. "She did, yes. He told her to get out of town. We followed his advice. I know Puri, been down here before. It's not too far from Calcutta. And the Z Hotel doesn't make problems about mixed couples checking in. No brainer, really."

Madhurima contemplated the situation. Becker strolled to the edge of the property where an unruly barrier — part fence, part young casuarinas and bushes — kept out the beach and the neighboring fishing village. A few seconds later he was back, casual, looking barely interested.

"But you must have known the police would come looking for you and Mrs. Roychowdhury?"

Richard looked at Madhurima with what she assumed was his helpless look. "Sure, but what else were we going to do? She didn't want to face the media. She told me by the time we got back, you guys would have caught the killer."

"Well, we haven't, Mr. Dunlop. That's why we have come all

the way to Puri. But presuming we will catch the killer, what are your plans?"

Richard emptied his glass and smiled into the milky afternoon sun that took its time setting over the Bay of Bengal.

"Well, actually, Paulami is so stressed. She told me earlier that she no longer wanted to see me. I don't know what to do now. I guess I might head south to Pondicherry."

Madhurima pondered that for a moment. She didn't like his self-assurance.

"Well, Mr. Dunlop. I wish you best of luck with your plans. For now though, you will stay put. And you may have to return to Calcutta with me for further questioning. I have taken your passport from the Z Hotel. I will return it in due course."

Richard looked at her angrily for a second, then he looked away and returned to his sunny disposition. "Sure, I understand."

Becker raised his eyebrows towards the street. It was time to go.

As they walked up towards the main road and the Z Hotel, Becker remarked, "Richard is lying. He almost lunged at you when you mentioned you were keeping his passport. Mrs. Roychowdhury isn't entirely truthful about everything either. Her brother-in-law is down here too, suggesting he wasn't straight with you either. No one connected to the killing of Abir Roychowdhury is straight with you."

"Do you think they are all in on the killing?"

Becker shook his head. "I can't imagine that. They all have such different agendas. But Roychowdhury had a lot of money if his wife could stay at the Oberoi."

"Money is always the best of motives," Madhurima agreed, "But what agenda does Richard have? I doubt she put him in his will for a few steamy nights at the Oberoi."

"He's a chronic freeloader," Becker answered.

Madhurima turned towards the sea. The sun was a red fireball, about to be swallowed by the wild expanse of the water.

Becker stopped in his tracks. In the last light of the day, his eyes reflected the sun's fire. He looked like a demon, but a good one at that. They stood in silence on the narrow road, the day's heat bouncing off the old crumbling palaces' white-washed walls. She could sense that he enjoyed the moment as much as she did. But something made her turn.

"Oh my god, it's Kishore up there on the main road. You follow him. He doesn't know what you look like. I will go and see an inspector I know here at the police station on C.T. Road, just in case I need back-up. We can meet back in the Z.'s lobby in an hour."

"What does he look like?"

"Tall, dark, handsome, and harassed. He just went off to the right. You can't miss him. He looks more cosmopolitan than most people in Puri. Please go."

———

Paulami almost jumped out of her chair when Kishore entered through the hotel's back entrance and crossed the casuarina garden to the terrace.

"What are you doing here? How did you know I was here?"

He carried a plastic bag with two cups.

"Paulami, my dear. That cop lady told me when she came to see me."

She stamped her foot on the tiles. How could everyone around her be so stupid?

"It didn't occur to you that this might be a trap?"

Kishore sat down, his old cheerful self. The man with whom she'd hatched the plan to kill Abir. The man who'd killed her husband. The man she thought she loved. Now she wasn't so sure anymore. Abir's death had unleashed strange, conflicting thoughts. She wouldn't miss him, but she was scared of what his death would bring her. True, his money was hers now. She was rich. Immensely rich. And Kishore had professed more than once that he would marry her. The rajbari would be hers too. In time. When the commotion had died down. But the commotion wasn't dying down, it was growing with every day.

"It doesn't matter. Did you tell them the Britisher went swimming on the day Abir was killed?"

"I did."

"They've probably arrested him by now."

Kishore pulled two cups from his bag.

"I bought some fresh lassi. Let's celebrate. The whole town is celebrating Rath Yatra. You should see the chariots."

She didn't feel like celebrating.

"Was it hard?"

Kishore looked like he had no idea what she was talking about.

"Was it hard killing Abir?"

"What are you talking about? I didn't kill Abir, I told you back at the house."

She laughed bitterly.

"I suppose some nameless goondas did him in, just for fun, by sheer coincidence on the day we had planned, in the location we had planned."

She took a sip of her lassi. It tasted rich, peppery. Thirsty, she gulped it down.

"So, if you didn't do as we arranged, who did?"

Kishore smiled at her. She'd never seen him smile like this before.

"Your toy-boy Richard. He did it. Who else could it have been?"

Paulami scoffed at the idea.

"Why would he do that? That's ridiculous. You're not making sense, Kishore. There's no one here listening. We don't have to stick to our story when it's just the two of us."

She stamped her foot down again. It felt different. As if the terrace floor had gone spongey.

"I mean, whatever. He will be arrested for it."

Kishore smiled savagely now. Paulami felt really strange.

"You cooked it all up. I know you did. You used that Britisher to kill my brother. You will go down for this, Paulami. Abir is no longer around to protect you. I already told the female cop that you were both at my house together, behaving like fugitives."

Paulami felt woozy and dropped her cup. She laughed, feeling a little spittle rolling down her chin.

"What are you talking about? We planned the perfect murder. Richard is our fall guy."

Kishore looked serious then, deadly serious.

"Remember we agreed, never change the story. But you changed the story. When I got to Bowbazar, there was no sign of Abir. But I did see the Britisher. I did see him closing an old wooden crate. That's when I knew, you'd changed the plan. You were planning to run away with that young man. You got him to murder my brother. You double-crossed me."

His features swam in front of her, in and out of focus. He still found him handsome, she had to admit, even as his skin began to emanate smoke, and his eyes turned orange. She tried to remember what he'd just told her. None of it was true. None of it made sense. She looked at her feet. They were far away. The cup lay on the tiles, a little lassi spilt. That's when she understood.

"You poisoned me."

He smiled, proud of himself.

"I really didn't think that would work. But it did. You never were the brightest star, were you Paulami? You really did think you could plan a murder with me, get someone else to do it behind my back and live happily ever after."

"The lassi…"

"Yes, enough opium to send an army to sleep. You see, Puri is a temple town. And because of the temple, the government runs bhang shops. And this afternoon I visited one, right near-by. And they didn't just sell marijuana. They sell opium. I bought a large chunk and took it to a sannyasi on the beach. He made me this brew, guaranteed to fell a buffalo, he said."

Kishore laughed. Paulami had to laugh with him. She didn't feel like laughing. But she laughed. And laughed. It was hysterically sad. She hadn't changed her story. How could it be going so wrong?

"When you got the boy to do the killing, I knew I was out of the game. No marriage, no money. Within a year, the banks will call in the loans for the hotel construction. I'll be ruined. But if you die, I'm the next of kin to Abir. You will die of grief and an opium overdose. You will throw yourself under the wheels of Jagannath, a grieving widow, no dependents, wanted by the police, shamed by an affair with a tourist, nowhere to turn. An everyday Indian tale of tragedy. So romantic, Paulami. Like Saptapadi, our favorite movie."

She didn't resist when he pulled her up gently from her chair and led her into the hotel, through the reception, into the garden and onto the street. She didn't mind when he put her into an auto-rickshaw and squeezed in next to her. The street was packed with pilgrims heading to the festival. The driver never let go of his horn, joining a thousand other horns, all blaring, all trying to go somewhere, even while stationary. When the traffic lightened, time contracted, and she was on a racecourse, doing a hundred miles an hour, her long black hair fluttering in the wind. She watched her hair turning into a flag, unfurled, her personal insignia for all to see. When they slowed back into a jam, time stretched to the milky horizon and became like the smoke rising from tea sellers' huts, thick, unhealthy and impenetrable. Paulami, she asked herself, where are you going, but then the thought was ripped from her mind, and she leaned back into her seat, cruising mindlessly towards the Jagannath temple.

The police had blocked direct access to the town's center. Paulami barely noticed when Kishore pulled her from the rickshaw and pushed her into the streaming crowd. People from all over the state, families and couples, groups of devotees and single old men were streaming into Puri to pay the respects to their god. The mood was festive. It was very hot. Kids were handing out plastic sacks filled with water. Rows of lepers vied for baksheesh. After an interminable amount of time, they emerged onto Trunk Road in front of the temple. The three chariots, transporting Jagannath, his brother Balabhadra, and his sister Subhadra, rose from an immense crowd a couple of hundred meters ahead of them. She barely understood what they were. They looked simply wonderful. Rising into the sky like temple roofs, decked out in bright red cloth, loaded with Brahmin priests and surrounded by a tight cordon of police in blue uniforms, the chariots were truly celestial vehicles. The gods were on their way to their aunt's house, the Gundicha Temple. How she wished to ride with the gods.

Paulami stood transfixed. Kishore grinned. She grinned, despite herself. The tropical sky was majestic and gun-metal grey. The crowd stretched beyond her vision. Groups of musicians, most of them drummers, danced wildly in circles. She watched their sweat flying off in all directions, absorbed by the sound of droplets passing her, hitting her shalwar, the heat and the crowds soaking her finally. She felt Kishore's hand on her back as he pushed her into the crowd, towards the chariots, towards the gods, towards heaven. She thought of Abir in his crate and laughed. And cried. Kishore's hand on her back started to burn and she took off leaving him behind. Then he was next to her again, sailing with her.

"Dying under the wheels of a chariot will bring you eternal salvation."

What he said was monstrous, but he was right of course. It couldn't be any other way. They passed the largest chariot carrying Jagannath, which formed the rear of the procession. Thousands of devotees heaved the huge wooden beast along, pulling thick ropes. The priests sat on the vehicle, weighed down by gold chains, garlands of marigold across their bare chests like bullet belts. She was going to have a good time with eternal salvation. They were altogether more handsome than Kishore or Richard. Definitely more handsome than Abir. The thought that her husband was no longer alive flashed through her like a jolt from an electric circuit cable. It didn't feel good. It didn't feel bad either, it just felt strong, so strong. Kishore was pushing again. They were between the first and second chariot now, between Subhadra and Jagannath. The crowd was surging forward. There was so much sweat. Thousands chanted "Jay Jagannath," over and over. The wooden wheels of the chariots were huge, some two meters in diameter. Wooden idols, brightly painted, waved at her from the vehicles' lumbering frames. The beasts seemed alive, breathing. She sensed that sacred pachyderms lived underneath all that red cloth. She remembered the ropes and the idea of elephants disappeared as quickly as it had arrived. Kishore was laughing again. The wheels moved. She was inside the cordon of police now. One of the main ropes was right by her side. She had heard, back there in another life, that touching the ropes was highly auspicious. She touched the rope. It was hard and sinewy. Whatever sweat a thousand devotees had left on it had been wrested from the fiber by the force of their pulling. The wheels were painted too. She longed to touch a wheel. The crowd chanted. Out of the corner of her eye, she saw a boy on a water tanker, a hose in his hand spraying a fountain of crystals into the crowd.

She felt Kishore's push. It wasn't hard. Just hard enough.

———

Madhurima and Becker watched Richard Dunlop emerge from his cell at Bowbazar Police Station. He was still cuffed, as was usually the case with foreigners who weren't prosecuted for a crime they had committed, but were being deported and banned from reentering India. The British Deputy High Commissioner began to berate Madhurima's boss, Assistant Commissioner Mazumdar, who made the cuffs disappear with a curt nod to Richard's guards. Everyone relaxed. There were handshakes. Richard spotted her and smiled.

"Sorry to ruin your romance. But mine didn't work out either," he hissed.

Then he was gone, pushed into a waiting car the British consulate had provided, which was headed straight for the airport. Wealthy parents, father a former diplomat, Richard was too important a man to ruin for a little murder that could be blamed on someone else. The British Deputy High Commissioner threw out his hand one last time and got into his own chauffeur-driven Mercedes. It was all over. Mazumdar walked over to her.

"I know what you are going to say. I listened in on your interrogation. Masterful. He did it, I'm sure. I believe Kishore's testimony. But we have no evidence."

"All we need is time. We will find something."

Mazumdar shrugged. "The Roychowdhurys are both dead. He was beaten to death by persons unknown, she threw herself under the wheels of a chariot. Case closed. That's what the British want. That's what we want."

"Kishore gets everything. I think they were all in on killing Abir Roychowdhury," Madhurima grumbled.

"Show me some evidence. Then you can nail Kishore, and you will have solved a case the city has been following at every step. Do your great uncle proud. If you fail, there's always night duty at Park Circus," he chuckled. "I'm joking of course."

Mazumdar disappeared back into the station.

Madhurima was frustrated. Everyone had been lying to her.

"What can we do?"

Becker had a glint in his eye.

"The only proof there might be of Richard being the killer is camera footage the Oberoi might have. If he's on camera leaving the morning of the murder, rather than lounging at the pool, then you have proof."

"But we're too late. Richard Dunlop is on the way to the airport. He'll never set foot in India again. And what was his motive?"

"He was keen on Paulami, perhaps on her wealth and status too. When he realized her and her brother-in-law were setting him up, he turned the tables."

"By being an even more malignant psycho than they are?"

"He wasn't going to call the police and explain himself."

"But we're too late."

Becker grinned. "I'm not sure. I can imagine that Kishore will also try and access that footage to clear himself. I mean, the wheels of justice are one thing, the media and a public reputation quite another. As you said, he got everything after Abir and Paulami die under unsolved circumstances."

"You're right, Kolkata society won't look kindly on Kishore Roychowdhury if no culprit is apprehended. But even if we establish that he scoured the footage, maybe even copied it, it doesn't prove anything. Nothing that would stand up in a court that is broadly sympathetic to men like him. This is India, he's a Brahmin and there's no evidence."

Madhurima flagged down a taxi and they slid into the back seat. It was worth a shot. For her own sake. And for the ten-minute ride with Becker through town. It was raining slightly. The air was warm and dirty, ready to be chopped into spongy blocks of unpleasant solidity. The traffic along Chandni Chowk was choking and the old Ambassador coughed and spluttered in tune with the rest of her city. Huge crowds swarmed around the Tipu Sultan mosque. She felt like touching his hand. Then she looked at him and knew it wasn't necessary. It didn't matter. The moment was theirs.

The Oberoi's security manager was flustered as he emerged from behind the long reception desk. His name tag read Jit Mondal.

"Good afternoon, Inspectress Mitra. Of course, you may look at the footage."

The man hesitated and tried to look elsewhere.

"What's the problem?" Madhurima pushed.

"Well, this is most awkward. We actually have another gentleman looking at the tapes, as we speak."

She saw Becker grinning out of the corner of her eye.

"In that case we will join the gentleman in his quest, whoever he might be."

Jit Mondal looked anything but relieved.

"You must understand. The hotel's reputation…"

She felt sorry for the man.

"It's Kishore Roychowdhury, isn't it? And he bullied his way in here with his high society connections. And he is rifling through your footage?"

The security manager said nothing and merely hovered. Behind him the hotel's GM had appeared. This was turning into a circus. She had to be very careful.

"Good afternoon, Miss Mitra. My name is Santanu Gupta." He handed her his name card. "I am the Oberoi's general manager. It's an honor to have you on the premises."

She could tell it wasn't.

"Will you take us through, please?"

Mondal, now ashen-faced, turned to his boss who finally brought himself to strut across the marbled lobby to formally greet Madhurima and Becker.

"Of course we cooperate with police investigations. Perhaps I may call your superior, just to check back on the propriety of your visit? It's Assistant Commissioner Mazumdar, isn't it?"

Madhurima smiled graciously. "It is indeed. But before you do that, I must tell you that the discovery of any untoward or unlawful proceedings under your prestigious roof could have consequences. You must be aware that the newspapers are covering my investigation in great detail, that my higher-ups have afforded me great freedom and that the case, at least in the eyes of our city's reading public, hasn't been wrapped up satisfactorily. How juicy an item of news the involvement of the city's most historic hotel would play out is your call."

The general manager gestured diplomatically.

"Please, Ms. Mitra, I will show the way. We hope that this can all be resolved with the minimum of fuss."

"I'm sure you do, Mr. Gupta," she said, emphasizing his name. "That way we can all go back to the business of fulfilling our respective roles in a professional manner in this great city — once we have checked through your footage."

Mondal's expression was a little pained. "I believe Kishore Roychowdhury has scanned through the footage. Mr. Dunlop did leave the property on the morning he checked in."

Santanu Gupta now wore an ingratiating expression.

"I may add, in order to assist the Calcutta police, that Mrs. Roychowdhury phoned her brother-in-law just prior to Mr. Dunlop leaving the premises."

"Do we know how long Mr. Dunlop was away?"

Mondal, after a confirmative nod from his boss, was just as eager to chip in. "Mr. Roychowdhury was just trying to establish this when you arrived and I was called out."

They followed Mondal behind the reception and through a bright back office to the security room. As they entered Kishore snapped around in a swivel chair. Richard was clearly visible on screen, from the back, entering the hotel's main door, which was held open by a towering Sikh in white livery. Kishore barely lost his composure and broke into a crude smile.

"Ah, Ms. Mitra and her foreign advisor. One last attempt at glory before they put you on traffic duty? I am going to the papers presently. The security footage shows that my sister-in-law's toy boy left the hotel around the time my brother was murdered. He was gone for almost 90 minutes Check for yourselves. Plenty of time to walk to Bowbazar, do the deed, and return to the Oberoi, don't you think? Imagine what an embarrassment this will cause? The hottest investigator on the force, the great niece of the city's great detective didn't think of checking the footage that determines that the killer's alibi was just a story?"

The door opened behind them. The general manager stuck his head in and nodded urgently at Madhurima.

"There's a call from Bowbazar for you, Ms. Mitra"

"That will be the proverbial ax falling then," Kishore laughed. "I'll step out into the lobby with you to see you crumble, if you don't mind."

She took the call at the far end of the reception counter. Assistant Commissioner Mazumdar was on the line. He sounded more animated than usual. Madhurima closed her eyes for a second, trying to ready herself for whatever was coming her way.

"Madhu, are you listening?"

Her boss had never called her Madhu. She felt insulted. It was all over. Mazumdar was going to humiliate her. Who knew who else was listening in on the call?

"Listen, every cop needs a bit of luck. Especially one who needs to crack a case that is as hard as the very foundations of our city. So, here's your life line. Act accordingly and with utmost authority."

"Yes, Sir."

Madhurima had stopped breathing. Becker was by her side. She could see that he had picked up on her distress. He would catch her if she fell, right here, right now, no matter the consequences. She swooned for a second, then pulled herself together.

"We just received the autopsy report on Mrs. Roychowdhury. She had so much opium in her bloodstream, she might well have passed out and possibly died in that infernal Orissa heat, had she not stumbled under the wheels of Lord Jagannath. I sincerely hope this will help you wrap up this sordid affair. I am scheduling a press conference for the morning. Now go and do what we're meant to do and prove this man is as odious as the city thinks he is."

Before she could say anything, Mazumdar had hung up. Becker couldn't have heard what her boss had said, but he'd pulled a bunch of photos out of his backpack and spread them theatrically on the reception counter. Kishore was closing in, still triumphant. The general manager and several receptionists craned their necks in a barely dignified manner. The entire lobby, chandeliers included, seemed to contract round Madhurima.

"He called me Madhu."

Becker grinned. Each shot showed Kishore, clearly and unequivocally, sitting in the government bhang shop in Puri, purchasing a fistful of opium. Becker had even managed to squeeze the shop's sign into one of the shots of Kishore handing over money, opium in hand. The date and time were marked on the images' bottom right corner. A couple of hours before Paulami had died.

Kishore had moved in and grabbed one of the images. He was pale as a ghost, but his composure quickly returned.

"Circumstantial. Anyone can buy opium in Puri. It calms my nerves."

"It certainly calmed your sister-in-law's nerves, didn't it, Mr. Roychowdhury?"

"You can't prove a thing."

"I just received the autopsy report."

Kishore turned his head. The Oberoi hadn't seen such a drama in years. Everyone was looking at him. In cold fury, he tore the photograph in his hands to pieces.

"It won't stand in court. Mazumdar will disown you."

She sighed inwardly with relief. If Kishore's connections didn't go higher than that, her boss had ditched him. Kishore was no longer protected.

"It was he who called me just now."

"You're lying," he spat. "I've known that man for years. Quid pro quo and all that."

"Are you going to risk that by defying me, or will you come with me back to the station without making a scene?"

Becker had pulled his camera from his pocket, pointed it at Kishore, a nice wide angle shot that took in most of the lobby, the staff and Madhurima and pressed the shutter. A sigh of anguish emanated from the staff.

Kishore hissed. "I own this city. I am one of the richest, most respected men in Calcutta. The boys in my neighborhood look up to me, Muslim, Hindu, or Christian. I encapsulate everything that is great about our beautiful Bengali culture. Just the way your great uncle did once upon a time. It's a shame the female side of the family doesn't have the same integrity and single-mindedness. Dwell on the fact that the Britisher killed my brother and that you let him slip away."

Madhurima laughed bitterly. "You are threatening me with the same under-the-table informality, the invisible hand of Calcutta, that let Mr. Dunlop slip out of the country."

She raised her voice ever so slightly. "But we have a case, my boss backs me up, our citizens will love it, and you are under arrest, Kishore Roychowdhury."

Madhurima loosened her hand gun in its holster, something she had never done on duty. The gesture was not lost on Kishore.

"You are ridiculous, Ms. Mitra. I will bury you and your legacy."

She sensed that he was almost done. His handsome face was covered in sweat despite the air-conditioned Oberoi climate. Becker took a short step towards Kishore.

"You're under arrest for the murder of Paulami Roychowdhury," Madhurima almost shouted. It felt like her voice carried all the way out onto Chowringhee and perhaps across the entire city, the proverbial last straw that broke the camel's back.

Kishore, incensed, lunged forward to slap her. Becker was there quicker and pushed him away. Kishore fell heavily onto hard marble, but he was up again in a second. Madhurima pulled her gun and repeated, "you are under arrest for the murder of Paulami Roychowdhury."

Kishore ran and was through the revolving doors in seconds. She didn't have the heart to shoot him. But she wouldn't let him go either. He great uncle had always told her that the mind was a detective's most powerful weapon. He'd been right, the mind was a fine investigative tool. But unlike her great uncle who'd been a heavy smoker, she'd spent half her life in the gym. Her strength was her weapon and hers alone. She holstered her weapon and stepped through the doors. The huge, Sikh guard pointed her in the direction Kishore had taken flight in, south, towards Park Street.

"Call my colleagues," she shouted at Becker and sprinted out of the hotel premises before grinding to an immediate halt. The crowd milling along the shopping arcade in front of the hotel was as dense as one could expect on a weekend afternoon. But Kishore was a tall man, and she could see him clearly, squeezing through the masses of people to her left. She wouldn't be able to catch up with him. He could disappear into New Market in seconds. She pushed through the crowd onto Chowringhee Road and started running. Within a minute, she was parallel to Kishore who was flailing through a throng of street vendors, shoppers and tourists. People looking for bargains didn't give way easily. She reached the next street corner, Humayun Place, before he did and she had her gun ready when he emerged and tried to duck into the small side street that led down to the New Empire Cinema.

Two uniformed cops had seen her, recognized her, and now formed a barrier either side of her. Kishore had nowhere to go. She raised her gun and fired in the air, just once.

"Kishore Roychowdhury, you are under arrest for the murder of Paulami Roychowdhury. If you try to flee again, I will shoot you."

———

The international departure hall at Dum Dum Airport was cold. Becker had checked in.

"I suppose I will call you Madhu, if your boss calls you Madhu. Since you offered."

"You can call me anything you like, Becker. I'm in your debt."

He smiled at her, and their eyes met, and this time it was no easier. It was probably the last time. It was as bitter as shukto, the bitter, gourd dish her mother used to make. She felt it all the way down in the pit of her stomach.

"Without your photos, we wouldn't have provoked Kishore into running. It was masterful. It may not be enough to convict him, but it was enough to draw him out and resist arrest three times. Assistant Commissioner Mazumdar told me we have a solid case. Public opinion is with us. He's under arrest, no bail, and in court for an initial hearing next month. He has money, so this will be a drawn-out case. But we did what we could."

Becker laughed. "No innocents in this case. Your first big case. Congratulations, Madhu. You're a star."

"We didn't catch Mr. Dunlop, the actual assassin. The prosecutor told us that they will pin Abir's murder on Kishore. They want it neat. Calcutta wants it neat. The British want it neat. The press will gobble it up."

"And that's why they want me out of the picture."

"Indeed," she sighed, surprised that she was on the verge of bursting into tears.

"It's ok," he said gently. "We will always have Calcutta. But just tell me one thing…"

She nodded, her eyes swimming.

"What's the name of that great uncle of yours, the man everyone in this town measures you against?"

"His name is Feluda. He called me this morning. He's so proud of me."

"What did he say?"

"He told me the city was changing, not for better or for worse, just changing. Twenty years ago, a man of Kishore's caliber might have beaten us and the case may never have made the courts. And a young woman investigator would have been thrown to the lions."

Becker picked up his camera bag and made a move for the

departure gate. She wanted to hug him, but her uniformed colleagues were around and for the moment, they all admired her.

"It's ok," he repeated, "we both know where we stand. Perhaps we'll meet again one day."

"I really hope so, Becker. Thanks for everything. You have a special place in my heart, always."

"That's what I wanted to hear."

With a last wave, he was gone.

PART TWO

KOLKATA 2019

'I sell mirrors in the city of the blind.' - Kabir

"Bom Bolenath. Bom Shiva."

The young sannyasi brushed his dreadlocks out of his face and held his chillum ready to be lit by one of his disciples. His parents had named him Aubrey, but now he preferred to be known as Firangi Baba, the foreign sadhu. It worked well with the locals.

Aubrey had taken Kolkata by storm. Every night he held court in an abandoned mansion in Black Town. His ancestors had lorded over Bengalis from what they had called White Town, but Aubrey had crossed over. Not that it mattered. He had made a useful discovery. The servitude his peers had forced upon Bengalis a hundred years earlier was still around. The colonizers were gone, but the country's elite had ruthlessly made the British divide-and-conquer strategy their own. Authority was bestowed not by merit or achievement, but by one's social background or caste. And a middle-class European runaway was a dark horse who could temporarily fit in high, low, and in between on the social ladder. He could grow dreadlocks, don saffron cloth, not shave for a month, put a monkey on a chain, and become a saint.

Sitting cross-legged on the building's broken staircase, Aubrey scanned the night's crowd. Streetwise goonda slum kids and middle-class hipsters turned up to his broken rajbari in ever-increasing numbers. Tonight, there had to be close to a hundred. The moneyed kids from Salt Lake came to smoke up. The poor from the neighborhood came because they had nowhere else to go. A foreigner was a rarity on the mean streets of Kolkata, an exotic bird to be followed, discussed, admired. Adda, they called it, the Bengalese penchant for aimless, animated discussion. Children approached Aubrey, just to touch the hair on his arms. He was on to something.

Aubrey's brother Magnus, bare-chested, a saffron gamcha, a coarse cotton towel, around his waist, stood ready with the matches, but the honor of lighting Aubrey's chillum always went to the most recent disciple. Tonight, a dwarf with a beaten face had lined up to do the honors.

"Sir, you are telling us such great stories. Night after night. But are we to believe everything you say? India has many sadhus, some good, some bad, some free as yourself, others in jail. Do you have special knowledge for us?"

Firangi Baba nodded sagely, absorbed in his role, method acting his way to nirvana.

"Light my chillum, brother, and I will tell you a story that will grab you by the seat of your longi."

Aubrey had a friendly moniker for all comers. Everyone was a brother or a sister. As for his job description, he had no real idea what a sannyasi was. He knew he had to appear to have renounced materialism and to have dedicated his life to pursue esoteric quests. He had stashed his laptop and JBL speaker, but he'd held on to his smart phone. Everyone had a smart phone. One needed one to commune with the gods these days.

The dwarf stepped up. Magnus handed over the matches as if they were sacred objects.

"What's your name, friend?"

"My name is Raju, Sir," the dwarf proclaimed proudly.

"And why are you here, brother? Why have you come to see me?"

Raju held the matches with sufficient awe. Aubrey knew what was coming next. Raju's life story would form another piece in a sheer infinite jigsaw of terrible tales he'd absorbed day-in, day-out since he'd arrived in Kolkata.

"Sir, I come from a village 160 km north of here. We are poor, we have always been poor. In our village, if your family is not connected to a political party it has no muscle. No one has enough, so everyone is watching everyone else. The powerful and connected families squeeze the rest of us. One day when I was twelve, we were out, farming a zamindar's sugarcane field. My mother was left at home only. The neighbors, they are higher caste, broke into the house…there was a violent incident. Since then, my mother has a mental issue. Then my father had a brain stroke. My sister now looks after my parents, but she has kids of her own and is expected to live in her husband's home. The dowry she paid to her husband's family has ruined us further. She cannot leave our dear parents, and I cannot leave the city because only I send money back home."

Aubrey looked at Raju with what he hoped was sufficient sympathy and respect.

"And what do you do to send money, Raju?"

The man's chest filled with pride when he heard the foreign sadhu repeat his name in front of the small crowd.

"I am a pick pocket. I am very good. I work around New Market. It is so very crowded there that a small man is not noticed. I send money home every month."

"Why don't you go back and look after your parents?"

Raju shrugged. "And who will earn money then? My sister's husband's family is just as poor as we are."

"Why don't you move your parents to the city?"

"They cannot leave the village. I have only one small, small room here. I don't want to go back. Life is better in the city because people don't know each other. In the village everyone knows everything about everyone else and the strong always use any advantage over the weak. That is the story of India."

The lesson of the dwarf's outpouring wasn't lost on Aubrey.

The little man continued. "I once spoke to an Australian man. I asked him how far away his neighbour's house was. He told me that if he shouts loud enough, his neighbor will hear him. Here in India, my neighbor is as far away from me as you are now, Sir. And he will watch me and if he is stronger than me, because of his caste, his job, or his income, he will take advantage of it."

Aubrey wasn't in Kolkata to provide a social service. He was no Mother Teresa. He merely wanted people to feel some hope. A tall order offering hope to a man less than four foot eight when there was none.

Raju stepped up, every movement steeped in deference and lit Aubrey's clay pipe. The ganja glowed for a second, then thick smoke enveloped the foreign sadhu's head, which all but disappeared. The crowd gasped. Aubrey smiled beatifically through the haze. He knew how to smoke that thing without going into a raging coughing fit. His expertise put the crowd on his side. Not only was he foreign, and perhaps wise, for the middle-class drop-outs he was also cool. For the rest, he was theatre. And theatre was what it was all about in Kolkata, a city of grand gestures and grander promises.

"Brothers and sisters, let me tell you a story," was how Firangi Baba began every night.

If nothing else, Bengalis loved a good story. Whether it was true or not hardly seemed to matter. But a few, lost souls that washed up on the banks of the Hooghly, swept into the city from across the vast plains of the subcontinent and desperate for an end to their journey, were ready to hear life-changing visions.

––––––

"You're homesick for a place you've never been to."

The old man gazed wistfully at Becker out of a beautifully restored art deco armchair.

"That's what they're like, both of them. This here..." he gestured towards the window and the world beyond, "...has never been enough for them. Can't think for the world what we might have done wrong to instill them with so much..."

He didn't finish the sentence.

Becker took a swig of the fresh pear juice, the best in the region he'd been told, and took in the view across the spires of Oxford, which stretched in medieval fashion across the horizon. He was communing with the gods among the city's movers and shakers. The old adage that it was lonely at the top had never rung truer.

"You come highly recommended."

Becker turned back to his potential client.

"Tell me about your problem."

The old man pulled two A4-size photographs from his desk drawer and spread them in front of Becker.

"Aubrey, 19, and his brother Magnus, just 18, have up and left for India. We took them there on a family holiday, many years ago. They loved it. So, they decided to go back there. Alone."

Becker said nothing.

"I can hear your thoughts across the table, young man. But please hear me out."

Mr. Bilham-Rolls rummaged in his drawer again and retrieved a pipe. It was filled and ready to go. He spent some time starting it up before he continued. Becker's father had smoked a pipe, many years ago. He recognized the tobacco's aroma, Erinmore, which conjured up images of his old man in another newly upholstered armchair, cleaning his pipes. The Erinmore tobacco company boasted to have produced the first pipe tobacco made of plants entirely grown in the British Empire.

"You see, they had a privileged childhood. I'm a lawyer, for one of the city's oldest firms. My wife inherited this house from her parents. The children had everything they could ever have wanted, including loving, caring parents."

A shadow crossed his face then, or perhaps it was his tone that changed.

"My wife died in a car accident three years ago. Since then, Aubrey's had visions about India. He was also involved in a serious car accident himself. I had to pull some strings to head off a trial. He's been arrested twice for possession of drugs, marijuana, and crack cocaine. I mean, who smokes cocaine in Oxford? He's been to see a psychiatrist, not entirely of his own volition. It was the only way to keep him out of prison. It has cost me some of my hitherto spotless reputation."

Mr. Bilham-Rolls put a particular emphasis into his last words, put his pipe out, and helped himself to a generous glass of pear juice from the glass jug on a wooden stand that looked like it had been made for the purpose. He raised his glass and looked at Becker directly. His expression was unbearably sad.

"Magnus, my younger son, is highly entrepreneurial. He sold Aubrey the crack. They've been gone three weeks. Three days ago, he sent me a photo on WhatsApp. A photo of Aubrey, disguised as an Indian mendicant, surrounded by a crowd who look like his disciples, in some kind of ruined fortification. An incredible photo. Absolutely shocking. The caption read, 'We'll be back when we've made our first million.'"

"Do you have the image here?"

The old man opened his desk drawer again and laid another printed A4 sheet in front of Becker. He was right, the photo was pretty impressive. A young westerner in sannyasi saffron robes had gathered a crowd around him. Boyishly good-looking, a little pale and out of it. He'd picked his stage well, a raised platform in front of an old mansion on the banks of a river. The skeletal shape of an iron bridge could be glimpsed crossing the water in the far distance. Becker knew the river well. He'd crossed the bridge, on foot, in buses, and taxis, many times. He had a pretty good idea where Mr. Bilham-Rolls' son was holding forth.

"I think they're trying to start a cult or something. Aubrey's visions, his outfit. Magnus's plan no doubt."

"They're in Kolkata."

"My God. That's where my wife died."

Becker let the ripples of the old man's words fade before he spoke.

"I'm sorry to hear this, Mr. Bilham-Rolls. But surely you understand that your sons have the right to travel to Kolkata and do whatever they want there so long as they don't break any local laws or don't get caught breaking them."

The old man sighed and leaned back in his armchair.

"That's why I didn't contact the consulate over there. I've explored the possibility of sending some ex-military guys. I know, I know. It sounds over the top. Then I heard of you. Of your expertise helping troubled youth in foreign countries. Aubrey has a deluded self of destiny, and he does what his younger brother tells him. And that's the terror of it. Magnus thinks he can live up to his father's expectations without going to university, without getting an education. He thinks it's all about the money, how much money he can make."

Becker looked sympathetic.

"Unless they get into trouble, there's not much anyone can do for you."

"Mr. Becker, perhaps I did not express myself properly. My older son Aubrey has visions. I think of them as delusions. He does not. Magnus has had some success suppressing his brother's visions with drugs. A very dubious success, if you ask me."

The old man rose to his feet abruptly, apparently not entirely averse to the odd theatrical gesture.

"Mr. Becker, I'd like you to check on them, tell them I want them to come home. And if they are in trouble, to help them. Just let me know your rates. If you bring them back, I double your fee. My sons are in danger. I can feel it. Please go to Kolkata and find them."

Becker thought it over. He felt like a private detective getting a job from a rich client, as he sat sweating in the old man's stiflingly hot office. It wasn't the kind of job he usually took on. But the money would be great and he could just go to Kolkata, track the boys down, and send a report.

"If I agree to this, then you need to understand that I will not pressure your children into coming home. I will tell them that this is your wish and that you're extremely worried. If they're fine, in the very widest sense of the word, and that to my mind in that age group includes self-exploration in far-away lands, then I will have fulfilled my side of the job."

The old man swallowed.

"And if not? If something is wrong?"

"Depending on what it is, I may have to involve local authorities to sort it out. I really can't say. I will do my best to make sure they are safe within the usual parameters most of us agree on."

"Name your price, Mr. Becker. It cannot to be too high if your swift engagement and assistance can help me sleep in peace."

Becker offered Mr. Bilham-Rolls his hand. It was time to go. The old man had a hard, dry shake.

"If you hire me, it's on an exclusive basis. I always work alone. I don't want any interference or competition from third parties. And definitely don't send any muscle. No ex-military. That kind of thing never goes down well in India. Or with me."

Bilham-Rolls nodded solemnly in agreement.

"How soon will you leave for India?"

"As soon as I can get a visa and a flight. Day after tomorrow I should think. Send me those images, copies of your children's' passports, any other information related to their travels."

The old man nodded, relieved and shattered at once. He waved weakly as Becker left the study.

———

"This city smells like the inside of a dog's mouth, Aubrey. How much longer are we going to stay in Kolkata? I am sick all the time. I scratch all night. I feel like I have millions of small animals living on me."

Magnus looked miserably at his brother. The afternoon heat was infernal. Even so, some of their disciples had already arrived at the abandoned mansion and were scrambling to find a shady place to sit. One man had collapsed at the foot of the stairs. Perhaps he'd died. Everyone had time. If only one could buy time, Aubrey thought.

"Call me Firangi Baba. The more we stay in character, the quicker we get what we want."

"It's just you who's in character."

Aubrey smiled benevolently.

"You just figure out a way how we make a fortune out of this. And I keep building, bringing in punters."

Magnus looked at his brother with a sour expression. "Monetizing on a bunch of starving homeless people isn't exactly promising."

"We wouldn't be the first ones to do so. Mother Teresa got a sainthood for exploiting the poor. And they still love her."

Magnus thought about that.

"If we were to start an ashram or some kind of spiritual center, we would need help from local people. And they will take a cut and quite possibly take us for a ride. A dead prophet is just as good as a live one. We need to plug into the hipsters who come to hear you speak. They have money."

"You're right, Magnus. Teresa is old school. We're the future. We don't need a spiritual center. We can be the Uber service for spiritual seekers. We provide nothing; they do all the heavy, esoteric lifting, and we get all the cash. We'll put Kolkata on the map. Eat your heart out, Silicon Valley."

Magnus lit up at the thought. "We will run a vlog, a YouTube channel, and a Twitter account. We'll be on Instagram and snapchat and every other online platform. You'll be the world's greatest spiritual influencer. So, you better come up with a cracking story that will reverberate beyond the spec of dirt we currently sit on."

"I have an idea, brother," Aubrey intoned. "I have an idea. Papa will be proud of us. He was always fond of a good scam."

As the sun dropped into the Hooghly river, the stairway of the mansion was packed. The police had shown up. Aubrey smiled. They were no longer alone. The poor had grown in number, a few had even lit a fire and were cooking dhal and making roti. The dwarf was back. The hipsters too had brought more friends and were smoking up, getting high and tuning in. A couple of bearded guys in trendy T-shirts and jeans were setting up a camera on a tripod. The more people who came to witness and record Aubrey's visions, the better.

They were ready to go.

Firangi Baba invited Raju to sit beside him. The dwarf was deeply touched, his lined face lit up and he scrambled to get close to his prophet. Firangi Baba got up and scanned the evening's crowd.

"Brothers and sisters, India is the richest nation on our planet. I'm not talking about your wonderful spirituality, your amazing cultural architecture, your incredible ability to fashion something out of nothing, your amazing food." He made a sweeping gesture across the gathered crowd — almost a hundred people, almost all men.

"Of course, India is rich, and yet it is full of poor people. That's because there's this long history here of the rich stealing from the poor."

Firangi Baba stopped theatrically. He'd worked out that if he spoke slowly and simply, most of his followers understood something.

"I have to tell you, brothers and sisters, that I come from England. My ancestors, the Britishers, arrived in Kolkata in 1690.

In those days, it was the East India company, the world's largest corporation at the time. A hundred years later we ruled West Bengal. When we first arrived in India, the country produced and provided more than a third of the world's goods and services. The East India Company plundered your country and looted your resources. By the time we left, your country had been pillaged by us."

The hipsters had stopped gossiping. Aubrey was a good orator. He had their ear. All eyes and cameras were on him.

"After independence, Kolkata stagnated, economically and culturally. I see the scars of this stagnation every day. This very palace is a symbol of it. But just around the corner from here, there's another kind of palace that never stopped making money."

The mansion was dead silent. Only the car horns on the main road, the city's ever-present soundscape, intruded on the gathering.

"Today is a great day for India. I stand before you with great humility. The white man has taken so much from your country, your politicians and landowners did the same after independence. Now it's time for you to take a small slice back. And those of you who find the key to your wealth — your enormous, incomparable wealth — will be rich beyond belief. As rich as the Nawabs."

The congregation held its collective breath.

"Anjezë Gonxhe Bojaxhiu."

Firangi Baba let the words stand and fall all by themselves, without explanation or anecdote attached. Raju was ready with the chillum. A second later, the white ascetic's head was enveloped in a cloud of smoke. He had spoken. They had listened. They would be back, and they would bring their friends.

Firangi Baba got up, put his hands together in momentary supplication, and stepped back from the stairway into darkness.

Magnus approached his brother with practiced deference and a couple disheveled hipsters in tow.

"Baba Ji, I want to introduce you to these fellow travelers on our great journey. Gaurav and Roni have been following your recent proclamations. They are film makers. They want to bring your message to a larger audience."

Firangi Baba smiled at the two men and gestured a warm welcome.

"You have been filming my talks. I am so happy. Perhaps we should pool our resources to take my message to a larger audience."

The younger of the two men, a squat man with a round head held together by a Rajput moustache, a three-day stubble, and a sly grin, answered, "We're shooting a documentary on the role of foreigners in Kolkata. We'd like to make you one of our main protagonists. You are such an enigmatic man; you are born to lead, and this city needs leaders."

Firangi Baba bathed in the shallow compliments. He was woozy after his smoke. And he'd forgotten their names as quickly as he'd heard them.

"What's your name, brother?"

"My name's Gaurav. And this is Roni. We're film makers. We're planning for a feature film about the city's poor. We've got our script. Like a Shantaram kind of thing. We have some actors lined up. We need to raise a budget only, so we're shooting this documentary to get the right profile."

Roni lit a bidi and grinned through his thick, greying beard. "We like your story, where you are taking it. I mean, we know what you're up to."

Magnus interrupted politely. "What in your opinion are we up to, Roni? We're just spreading a message of compassion. That's all."

Gaurav coughed and pulled a packet of Gold Flakes out of the pocket of his grimy white shirt. "Mother Teresa. You've been hinting at her every night. You and your visions. You're going to tell these poor souls that she was rich beyond belief? That they should storm her missions?

"Please don't smoke cigarettes in my presence, friends."

Gaurav was surprised, perhaps offended, but he put his smoke back in its box.

"I detect a certain hint of sarcasm in your comments. You doubt my visions. I had noticed you, coming here, filming me. I am always happy to welcome like-minded souls, but I have no time for doubters. I was hoping you'd get with the program."

Roni, his voice dripping with false humility, asked, "and what benefit do your disciples derive if they get with your program, Firangi Baba? What reason might there be for myself and Gaurav not to cut a short clip for the local news channels about a white raja lording it over us poor Bengalis? We lap that kind of stuff up like nothing else. You'd be in a Kolkata prison cell before the evening news."

Raju sidled up to the two filmmakers and pulled at Roni's leg. "Firangi Baba has visions. I have seen it with my own eyes."

He pulled a small but sharp looking knife from his rags and made a slashing movement across the back of Roni's thighs.

"You make trouble for Firangi Baba and I find you and cut you. I am small. You never see me coming."

What was left of the crowd closed in on the tense group. Magnus threw his arms up in mock exasperation.

"Friends, there's no need for threats. Firangi Baba's message is one of empathy. And you guys have been here every night, taking it in, filming it. Let's work together and bring this message to the world and we will all benefit."

"Let's," Gaurav laughed darkly.

———

Becker's flight landed at Netaji Subhas Chandra Bose International on time. He was pleasantly surprised that the erstwhile Dum Dum Airport had been given more than a facelift. It was a whole new game. The immigration officers were as grumpy as ever, but the arrivals hall was bright, cool, and almost silent. Would the city also have changed beyond recognition? Would the biryani still be good? He'd been back to India many times since his first trip twenty years earlier. The country had developed at lightning speed, edging away from its cultural particularities, globalizing at a speed only the gods could measure, for better or for worse. But he'd never been back to Calcutta.

As he stepped out into the sweltering afternoon heat, a small part of him was hoping to see Madhurima Mitra. Of course, they hadn't spoken in twenty years, she didn't know he was coming, and there was no reason to contact her that wouldn't have made him feel creepy. He had no idea whether she was still a police officer, or even if she was still alive. But whatever else Becker was going to do here, he was going to find out.

An hour later, he was back in his old room at the Broadway. Here, time had virtually stood still. The owners had changed, but the lift operator merely looked older, and one could no longer smoke in the bar. Outside on Chandra Ganesh Avenue, the traffic was almost as bad as in any other Asian metropolis, and Uber was all the rage. Some of the pavement dwellers, or their children, were still around. The yellow Ambassador cabs, he knew, were no longer being manufactured. They remained plentiful, coughing up and down the city's potholed streets. But they were on the way out. The city had changed its name since his last visit. It was Kolkata now. But as he gazed from his balcony down into the street, he felt good about being back, good about being alive in the here and now. Becker had no idea what awaited him and that was just as well. Promise was better than certainty, that had always been his motto. Now that he'd just turned 45, was single, gainfully employed, and unburdened by responsibility, this had never been more pertinent.

An hour later, Becker emerged from the Kolkata Metro at Shobhabazar, the heart of what had once been Blacktown, the northern part of the city where the rich traders and zamindars, who had helped the British exploit their own people, had settled in fantastical mansions. He didn't need to check the photograph of the young Bilham-Rolls to figure out their exact location. He had a good idea where they were. He headed west towards the river.

Becker was happy to see that Kolkata continued to cherish some of her old grand dame airs. While the main road was lined with shops selling air-conditioners and trendy hair dressers, the narrow lanes that led to the Hooghly harbored traditions and lifestyles that, for better or for worse, hadn't changed in decades. Becker had been following the city's trajectory from afar. The old political structures, the communists, the TMC under Mamata Banerjee, had burnt themselves out. He spotted their flags and emblems on every wall, but those were old walls and old flags. People were tired of the old because the new was being withheld from them, even as it was just beyond their reach, perched and waiting for its moment. There was a general expectation of relief — the old Bengali elite was sick of the ruling party's gangsterism and felt sidelined by imagined Muslim emancipation. The young street punks had neither perspective nor opportunity. The rich sent their children abroad. The educated left for other metros across India. The next election, or the one after, would go to India's far right nationalists. Development would come in its wake. Along with pogroms and political violence and further destitution, pollution and polarization. But people needed change.

Ten minutes into his ruminations, Becker crossed the railway lines and hit the road above the ghats that lined the river banks. The sun, a pale, weak fire ball, was just dropping into the waters behind a couple of decrepit ferries that plied the Hooghly, crowded with commuters. To the south he could see Howrah bridge throw its might across the water towards the city's main railway station. The ghats, the steps that led down to the water's edge, were busy with Hindu devotees, dhobi wallahs watching over clothes spread out to dry, kids hunting for entertainment, and a few mendicants who'd come to visit the Baba Bhutnath Temple, and perhaps to die there, just couple of minutes' walk away. They certainly looked as if that could have been a consideration. He passed a young woman in a beautiful purple sari, decked out in golden jewelry and felt a pang of longing. He'd never seen Madhurima in a sari. Perhaps, he thought, he should not get in touch with her. That way he would always remember her just like the woman he'd just passed — young, vivacious, and frozen in time. Surging crowds milled around the temple, either to say prayers or touch its giant Nandi, a silver bull, just inside the building, for good luck. Others had come to say farewell to relatives who arrived with unquestionable regularity in rickety hearses and were then carried into the Nimatala cremation ghat next door. Becker barely recognized the place, a series of intertwining chimneys, painted white and blue, the colors of the ruling TMC, that reminded him more of the Centre Pompidou in Paris than any place of death and rebirth he'd seen in India. It was said that Shiva, for whom the temple had been built in the 16th century, visited the burning ghats at night and covered himself in the ashes of the dead.

A couple of minutes farther south, Becker found what he'd been looking for: a property overgrown with bushes, its walls split by roots and vines, an old zamindar mansion crumbling amidst dusty foliage. In the evening gloom, he could barely make out the narrow path through the mini-wilderness but he pushed on anyway. A very short man, a dwarf, sidled up to him and shook his head the way people did in India.

"My name is Raju. You are a friend of Firangi Baba?"

Becker looked down at Raju and smiled. "I am a messenger."

The dwarf looked at Becker doubtfully and then shrugged his crooked shoulders.

"I take you to him."

Raju pushed ahead through unruly bushes and piles of garbage until they emerged in the mansion's horseshoe-shaped courtyard that opened onto its own ghat and the river. A couple of torches had been lit at the top of a broken staircase. A crowd had gathered at the foot of the stairs. Becker noticed a camera crew, street kids smoking chillums, and a gaggle of middle-class youth — beards and girls in cotton fashions clutching funky handbags and smart phones. The rest of the gathering was made up of the wandering and insane. A pretty inclusive crowd.

Raju gestured for Becker to descend. The stairs were clearly reserved for someone else.

He had barely sunk into the crowd when the Bilham-Rolls brothers made their appearance. Magnus showed up first, barefoot, dressed only in a saffron gamcha, his face behind a clay mask. He carried a wooden stick and did his best to look imperious. The mud on his face helped a little. Becker had him down as an Apocalypse Now freak. The crowd went silent. The sounds of the city receded.

Firangi Baba appeared in the center of the stairway. Aubrey Bilham-Rolls 2.0 cut a dashing figure. His matted hair fell across his face like the snakes of the Medusa. He was bare-chested and dressed in a gamcha, like his brother, but he was clearly the main player on their improvised stage. A macaque on a chain trailed behind him. Raju stood close-by. Becker was impressed. Jack Sparrow had nothing on this kid.

"Brothers and Sisters, I want to see a sea of hands out there."

The crowd, at least those who'd understood what he'd said, raised their hands. Firangi Baba had impeccable timing. He waited until everyone had settled down before he continued.

"Brothers and Sisters, I want to tell you a story. A true story."

Becker looked around. Most people around him looked like repeat customers. They were here every night, hoping to be spun a tale, true or not.

Firangi Baba continued. "You all know Mother Teresa: Kolkata's great saint. You all know she died in 1997 and that she ran Missions of Charity all over the world. Those charities run schools, orphanages, soup kitchens, mobile clinics, and so on.

Mother Teresa was a tireless fundraiser, and throughout her life she met heads of state and private companies to ask for donations. But she never built modern hospitals. Her homes lacked proper medical care, the food she offered those who stayed was often inappropriate, the painkillers given to the very ill were insufficient, and there were no doctors on hand for proper diagnosis. Since her passing, many people have asked what happened to all this money, those millions in donations that she received to help the poor and dying. The answer to that, my friends, is that no one knows."

He paused and scanned the crowd. He briefly made eye contact with Becker and looked surprised, confused even. Magnus stepped up beside his brother.

"Firangi Baba can open doors. Doors that lead to heaven or hell, salvation or death. Come back tomorrow night. He will tell us what happened to the hidden treasures of Teresa."

Raju stepped up with a chillum and offered it to Firangi Baba. The young man sat down, took the clay pipe, and gazed at his congregation. The dwarf stepped up and lit the marijuana. The young sadhu's head disappeared in a cloud of smoke. By the time the smoke had cleared, Becker had climbed the stairway and stood facing the young man.

"Aubrey Bilham-Rolls. Thanks for a lovely evening."

Firangi Baba looked at Becker a little uncertainly. A sly smile might have crossed his face, but Becker wasn't sure the white holy-man registered him properly.

Becker continued to speak slowly and clearly. "I was sent here by your father to see if both of you are ok."

But he only reached Firangi Baba, not the young man underneath. Magnus and Raju crowded into Becker from behind.

Aubrey's younger brother hissed. "The dwarf's got a blade, and he will stick you with it if we tell him to. You're not wanted here. We don't need to talk to you. Everything has changed. We're free," he grabbed Becker's shoulder, not too gently. "Perhaps it's good that you came. Tell the old man that we won't be back, whether we make our million or not. We're sannyasi, we have given up our old useless identities. And don't come back or Raju will sort you out."

Raju flashed a knife at Becker. His earlier charm had vanished. He looked sufficiently sycophantic to stick Becker with his blade. Becker tried to make eye contact with Firangi Baba, but the older boy's face was empty and withdrawn, stuck on something more potent than the cheap weed he'd been smoking in public. Becker smiled and retreated into the thinning throng of devotees. He was happy. He'd made contact.

He made his way down to the water's edge. Plastic garbage and a dead, bloated cat floated by. Howrah Bridge shone above the river like Godzilla's ribcage. Neon lights reflected off the water, and the sky was an unearthly orange. Close to the crematorium, the river smelled awful. The blue hand of Kali, a broken piece from a statue that had been immersed in the river months earlier during the festival celebrating the city's fierce goddess, rose from the muddy ground, a strange, lonely gesture of rebellion.

He heard a chain grating on stone and turned. Raju and the monkey were coming down the broad steps towards the water. Becker tensed, ready to run. He didn't fancy getting stabbed by the little man and bleeding out on the banks of the Hooghly. But Raju kept his distance and moved his head in the expected fashion. "I will not hurt you. It's just Firangi Baba's brother. He doesn't like outsiders. No one too close to Baba Ji. Baba Ji has visions."

Becker said nothing.

"You work for the father of Firangi Baba."

"He wants me to bring his children home."

Raju looked wistfully out across the water.

"You have to wait. They are not ready. They have to tell their story. Firangi Baba's visions. The people want to hear them. More and more every day."

"He had these visions back home. The doctors said he was sick."

Raju smiled without happiness.

"I know. But it doesn't matter. And his brother will never go back."

"What drugs is he on?"

"Fin," Raju answered. The monkey started pulling on his chain.

"Opium?"

Raju nodded.

"Why are you talking to me?"

The little man smiled sagely.

"These two brothers don't belong here. You Britishers don't belong in Kolkata. I have two children, back in my village. I almost never see them. So, I understand. My life is always the same. Firangi Baba is good to me."

Becker agreed.

"I will hang around and wait, as you suggest, Raju."

"Good. We find Mother Teresa's money, and then you go."

Becker cringed inwardly.

"I know what you are thinking. But you are wrong. In India we know what is wrong can be right. And what is false can be true. And what is imagined can be found."

Becker wrote his name, address, and phone number on a slip of paper.

"Call me if something changes. Otherwise I will be back tomorrow."

Raju let the macaque pull him back towards the mansion.

"Make sure Magnus does not see you. Otherwise I have to stick you with my knife."

———

Firangi Baba lay back on the rickety charpoy, the traditional Indian string bed, which stood in an otherwise empty cell behind a truck driver's dhaba in Shobhabazar, a stone's throw from the river. It was all they could afford.

Magnus had the tin foil spread out and was cooking up a small chunk of opium. He never touched the stuff, but there was always some for Aubrey. Getting more wasn't a problem. Kolkata was saturated with cheap drugs. Every street corner hustler, and there were more than a few, had something to sell. And the opium Aubrey had been smoking was doing the trick. He was having visions, shaking all over, going hot and cold, sweating through his gamcha, but now he was slowing down.

"Aubrey, relax. You know they will pass."

Firangi Baba looked at Magnus without comprehension.

"Teresa's treasure. It's buried. I can see it now. She used oilskin."

"Aubrey…"

"I am Firangi Baba. You have to trust me. You of all people, have to trust me. I'm not making it up. I am in touch with mom. She is telling me things, every day. She told me about the oilskin."

Magnus snapped angrily. "Aubrey, mom is dead."

"I know. She died here in Kolkata. That's why it's such a trip to be back. Here, among all the cacophony, I can finally hear her clearly. I just need a little more time. But we're ok now, people give us food, medicine, more and more are coming every night…" He drifted off, out of it.

"They are all zombies. Or stoners."

"And the film guys. We will be famous when we find the treasure."

Magnus sighed. "The film guys want to screw us."

Aubrey looked at his brother as if across a great distance. They both knew he was burning out. Some people thrived in India; others shrunk. They would have to be quick. Magnus had told him that the easiest way to get people to notice an extrovert was religion. And technology was the key to getting noticed by the right people. The film guys, the YouTube channel. The revelations to come.

He watched his brother for a while, the slowly turning ceiling fan providing the only soundtrack, a kind of symphony of creaks and grinds, with the stale, cold smell of cheap heroin lingering in their rotten room.

Magnus got up and walked out. Aubrey waited for what seemed to be a lifetime. But Magnus didn't return.

———

Becker was enjoying a late afternoon beer, his first, when she walked in. It was just like the first time. But of course, it was very different.

"Hi there. You're Becker?"

Becker was stunned. He almost dropped his glass. Madhurima towered over him, the way she had twenty years ago. She looked young, vivacious, like she meant business. The same black hair tied up in a bun, similar clothes, the same flawless skin, though she had several metal studs in her ears and a small geometric tattoo on her wrist. He looked around; the Broadway's bar was the same it had ever been. He felt disoriented, like a victim of time travel. He got to his feet and shook hands. Her touch was warm and not quite soft.

"Please, sit down. Would you like a drink? Who are you?"

The young woman took the chair opposite Becker.

"I'll take a small glass of your beer only. If you don't mind."

"You're not on duty?"

She laughed pearly teeth.

"No, I'm not a cop. My name is Devi. I am Madhurima's daughter."

"Wow,' was all he could say.

The young woman shot him a self-confident smile. Her dark

eyes, embedded in thick layers of kohl, shone like bottomless pools.

"You look the way I remember your mother. I haven't seen her in twenty years."

"Yes, she told me. "

He didn't ask what else Madhurima had told her daughter about him.

"I guess it's not a coincidence you're here."

Devi smiled and took a sip of beer.

"No, Becker, it's not. Mum is working on a kidnapping case. A witness passed a piece of paper to her, with your name, address, and phone number on it. She's busy with her bosses. I think she is under pressure. The kidnapped kid has wealthy parents. That's all I know. So, she sent me. Told me it would surprise you."

She looked at him a little strangely then.

"You look like a nice man, Becker."

He didn't know what to say, so he kept quiet and tried to get his social skills to kick in.

"It's fantastic to meet you, Devi. Such an honor. And huge surprise. So great to meet Madhurima's daughter. I had no idea."

"That's because you two haven't spoken in like twenty years, right?"

Becker nodded.

"I suppose she is Commissioner now?"

Devi shook her head. "Come on, man, mom is the real deal. She's still inspectress. She refused flat out to be promoted. She's the city's best investigator. And you really helped her back then with that infamous Roychowdhury case."

Becker tried to remember how it had ended.

"Did the brother go to jail?"

Devi looked at him a little impatiently.

"Think you better ask mom about all that. That was your time, guys, right?"

Becker ignored the question.

"What would Madhurima like me to do?"

"You need to wait here, Becker. Mum will come and pick you up this evening."

Devi got up to leave.

"Thanks for the drink, man. Wouldn't have missed this for the world. Becker, you're a legend. She never thought you'd be back though. And this is just such a weird way to be back in touch, 'ey? I mean, married through crime or something?"

Becker couldn't quite read the young woman. She was cocky, and he was unsure of himself. He relished the moment.

"Am I a suspect?"

"You always were, Becker, I've been told," she winked at him and was gone.

Becker was on his second beer and a plate of dhal makhani when a uniformed policeman waved for him from the door. Outside, the sepoy directed him to a white Ambassador parked by the curb a few doors west of the Broadway.

He slipped inside. The driver saluted him and took off into Kolkata's rush hour traffic. An hour later, the car dropped Becker by the Hooghly. It had gone dark, but that barely made a difference to the temperature. Another sepoy led him through the gates of the Nimatala cremation ghat. The police had marked off a few square meters of embankment. Becker recognized the shape that lay twisted on the concrete ramp that led down to the water's edge.

Raju lay in a puddle of dried blood.

"He bled out slowly. Someone cut the artery in his thigh. Welcome back, Becker."

"It's been a while," was all he could say. Then he tore his eyes away from Raju and looked at her. Her face had softened. Her hair was short. Something had hardened in her expression. The years had left the same traces he saw when he looked in the mirror in the morning. But the eyes were the same. They had the same glow, the same intensity, and the same affection. That's what upset him the most.

"Madhurima."

"Becker."

He wanted to hug her. She felt it and took a step back.

"Thanks to your assistance all these years ago, I made career. After solving that murder back then, they just threw every case file at me they could find."

"Sending you daughter to alert me was a trip."

"I thought it might be a nice touch," she laughed confidently. "After all, she could have been your child.'

"Had things panned out differently."

She smiled, her thoughts perhaps drifting back to their past, and then changed the subject.

"The victim, Raju, was well known in the area. Quite a popular and colourful character. I am told the foreign holy-man appeared and Raju took to him and became a sort of assistant, translator, and so on. No one in Shobhabazar disliked Raju enough to kill him. He didn't owe any money to the loan sharks. He was not addicted to brown sugar. He was not even in a gang. He didn't answer to any of the local dadas. He did have your number in his pocket though. Yours. Imagine my surprise. I recognized your hand-writing. So, after exhausting all other avenues of enquiry, I called for you."

Becker grinned. "Yes, that was a nice surprise. Bit of a shock actually."

She laughed at that. A little forced perhaps, but she laughed.

"I thought you might like the touch. I couldn't get away myself. I could have just sent a sepoy. But I thought the occasion demanded a little more," she touched his arm then. "And I owe you, Becker. After we cracked the Roychowdhury case, the media went crazy, thanks to me being the grand-niece of Kolkata's best-known detective. As you may remember. I was feted. They tried to kick me upstairs straight away, but I refused. So here I am, deeply entrenched, up to my knees in mud and blood, but happy to be doing real police work. In part, thanks to you. How have you been, Becker?"

It was his turn now to condense twenty years into three soundbites and he found himself struggling to furnish her with anything as concise. "Well, I'm ok. Thanks. After I left India back then, I went back to uni, studied psychology and Hindi. But then I got a job working with US military vets in Germany for a while — guys who'd come out of Iraq, shot to pieces. When that ended, I became a kind of foreigners-lost-in-India specialist. I visited often in the last ten years, usually working for rich parents looking for their absconding kids in India."

"Which is why you are back in Kolkata?"

Becker nodded. "Yes, for the first time since then. For the two brothers, Aubrey and Magnus."

"Magnus's been kidnapped, Aubrey's a mess, and Raju dies with your note in his pocket. You certainly make a great entrance."

She looked at him with the same shrewdness that he'd noticed in her back then, honed to a fine art in the twenty years since.

"Almost a bit too much of a coincidence."

He gestured disarmingly. "Same as last time: wrong time, wrong place. Except now it's my job, back then it was holidays."

"Well, Becker, I won't have you arrested, but we got your C-form from the Broadway, and you will have to give me your passport."

He was genuinely happy to see Madhurima, but he'd noticed straight away that her tone was a little strained. She looked conflicted, if one dug past her exceptionally professional demeanor.

"What's your assignment?"

"The father of the boys asked me to make contact, tell them to return home, and in the event that they run into trouble in India, create circumstances that will allow for their repatriation."

"Is that the case now, Becker?"

He nodded grimly. "I guess with one man down, one man

71

missing, and one man out of it, that's what the situation amounts to."

"Who is the father?"

"He's a rich lawyer, well connected. He dotes on his children and will do anything to get them back. I am just the first instance. If I fail, others will come. They will be more resolute and less accommodating."

"He pays well?"

"Yes, he does. More so if I return his boys."

"So, we better hurry, Becker. They are going viral on the net, and the wrong people are getting the wrong ideas about these kids. They call the older boy a prophet. Firangi Baba. It might catch on. India loves a godman, and he wouldn't be the first foreign one."

"I know, I met them both last night. I also met Raju."

Madhurima looked at him directly for a moment before she averted her eyes.

"We better keep that to ourselves."

"It's good to see you look so well, Madhurima. It's been a long time."

"Yes," she answered, struggling for the right words, "I thought often what you said back then, 'We will always have Calcutta.' So, this is confusing. But it's good to see you too. You have become a man. And I have become a mother. We have to make the best of it. Do you have children?"

Becker shook his head.

"Free as a bird."

"Oh," was all she said.

They left Raju to the police guards and the river crabs, and made their way to the mansion.

———

Firangi Baba had taken his usual position on the top of the mansion's stairway. Tonight, he was alone. He looked a little out of sorts at first, scanning the crowd, which had swollen to a couple of hundred men and a handful of women. Becker noticed that the two guys with the camera were not around. Following Madhurima, he made his way to the bottom of the staircase.

"Brothers and Sisters, I want to see a sea of hands out there."

Most of the gathered raised their hands. The devotees were becoming institutionalized.

"Some of you doubt me. Some of you believe that I have visions. Trust me, brothers and sisters, my visions are true. That's why my brother is gone, taken away by someone who means me harm. That is why Raju is gone and why the police are here tonight. There are those among us who have murder in their eyes and greed in their hearts. I am saddened by this. I want my brother back. I will not reveal the location of Teresa's treasure until my brother is returned to me, safe and sound."

A tired groan went through the white sadhu's audience. Everyone was hungry for knowledge. Some were just hungry.

"Brothers and Sisters, a good man was killed tonight. Bring me my brother or die without ever knowing what it means to be rich."

The crowd moved forward as one. Firangi Baba didn't move. The mood was turning ugly. Madhurima had sensed it as well. She nodded to Becker, and they climbed the stairway, putting themselves between the sadhu and his devotees. Becker positioned himself directly in front of the young man. But the gathered souls were too far gone to care. They started closing in, their faces angry, hissing curses under their breath.

"They are blaming foreigners for their misfortune. That includes you right now. I am calling for back-up," she snapped, phone in hand.

Becker kept his eyes on the men closest to him. They weren't going to stop. He had nowhere to run this time. A haggard thirty-something-going-on-sixty lunged for him. He stepped out of the way just in time, and his assailant stumbled on the stairs. The next three guys were already on the move, ready to trample their fallen compatriot to exact revenge. He didn't stand a chance. The three men looked determined and made their move. A gun shot ripped through the assembly. Becker ducked. The crowd panicked and dissipated in all directions. His three would-be attackers looked at each other briefly and melted back down the stairs and into the gloom. He turned to see Madhurima point her gun where they'd stood a second earlier. The mansion's courtyard flooded with uniformed officers. Firangi Baba had gone.

———

The first thing Magnus noticed when he came to was the smell. It was awful, a mixture of feces and death. He came awake quickly scratching his arms and chest. He was itchy all over. The boy in the corner looked at him without sympathy and left the low-ceilinged room they were in without a word. Shortly after, another youth entered. He looked dark and tough and had a small monkey chained to his shoulder.

"I am Dead King. I run this part of Dhapa. You want drugs, you want guns, you want someone kidnapped, you come to me."

Magnus didn't think the youth very bright.

"I've already been kidnapped. By you guys. I'm not here of my own will. Let me go. I have no money at all."

Dead King smiled sardonically. "But you do, Britisher. You know where Mother Teresa hid her money."

Magnus did his best sincere laugh and countered, "Why would I be staying in a ten-dollar room if I had access to a treasure. I'd be staying at the Oberoi, not in some Shobhabazar fleapit."

Dead King didn't look like he'd heard of the Oberoi.

"Why am I here? How did you find me? Why did you pick me?"

The young gangster laughed. "The whole city is talking

about your brother, babu. We are all waiting to hear about the location of Teresa's money. But it was Gaurav and Roni who asked us to kidnap you. The filmie guys. Torture you a little too if you don't talk. But they haven't paid up. So, for the moment, you will stay here."

An anguished scream pierced the stink in Magnus' temporary jail. A man cried and pleaded in Bengali. The voice sounded familiar. Dead King got up.

"We are talking to Gaurav only. I will be back when he has told us what he knows. Don't try to run, I have my boys everywhere, and they will cut you before you get to the main road. Remember what happened to Raju."

Magnus felt sick. One more night in this hovel and he knew he'd be dead. He'd always fancied himself as a hard man, but India was harder than most. He got up and realized his shoes were gone. He headed for the door in his socks, trying to fight nausea. Outside a pale sun shone tiredly across a muddy field surrounded by low walls topped by barbed wire. He took a closer look at the ground. It wasn't mud. He'd been abducted to the world's largest open-air toilet. He was standing in shit. A hundred meters or so away, he could see several new high-rises, including a Marriot and a couple of other luxury hotels. In the distance, half built multi-story buildings loomed out of the orange haze. The concrete shells looked like they'd already served their purpose and were on the way down, not up. It was bewildering. He'd been kept in a one-story, two-room box, constructed of bricks, mud, and tarpaulin. An old bed-spread had been laid out in the middle of this sea of shit in front of the building. Five boys were lounging on the dirty cotton, passing a skull-shaped bong. After a couple of hits, they probably felt like sitting on a magic carpet floating above the least salubrious corners of the known universe. He didn't really give a shit, there was already more than enough to go around for everyone. He laughed at his own pun. Dead King was sick. His kingdom was dead. Magnus needed to get out.

The boys waved for him. He gingerly waded through the detritus and stink. They offered him the bong. In the absence of breakfast and a cup of coffee, he didn't hesitate. He placed himself on the edge of their magic carpet and took a hit. The awful smell faded temporarily, replaced by the weed fumes and something else. A cold ripple moved down his spine.

The oldest boy, not a day past eighteen yet, laughed. "A little brown sugar in the morning only. To get you through the day."

He grinned uncertainly. Coffee was better. Dead King emerged from the second room wiping his bloodied hands on his longi.

"We will let you go. Gaurav too. It's like clapping with one hand, listening to you guys. By the way, Gaurav told me about a tall Britisher that is trying to stop you guys from revealing the location of the money."

Magnus thought hard. Gaurav meant Becker, the guy who'd been sent by his dad. He shrugged. Becker was expendable. Dad would just send more guys to get them if this one wasn't successful. Dad was persistent. Perhaps there was a way out after all.

"Yes, Becker, his name is Becker."

"He works with the cops?"

Magnus had no idea. "He does?"

Dead King nodded.

"And he is searching for Firangi Baba."

"Then let me go back to my brother. He needs me."

"Will he reveal the location of the money?"

Magnus lied effortlessly. Anything was good enough to get him out of here.

"He has visions. They have been pointing him in the right direction. But he needs to have more visions to reveal the details."

Dead King scoffed and took a hit on his bong.

"My boys will take you to the main road. We will deal with

the tall Britisher. You will find your brother, wait for his vision, and tell us where to go. If not, you will both come back here."

Magnus tried to look humble. But he was relieved. He needed to find Becker, tell him he had Kolkata's underworld after him, and have him extract Aubrey and himself as soon as possible. There was nothing to be gained from his brother's performance with so many people closing in. It was time to quit for better climes. With the old ways dying in Kolkata and the new not born yet, too many monsters were out to play.

———

Williams and Mathews had been waiting in front of the Marriot in Dhapa for more than an hour. Mathews was on this third cigarette, his handsome face lit up by neon reflection bouncing off a handful of luxury high-rises that had recently been planted in a sprawling wasteland of landfills and slums. The landfills had first been established by the British. Their odor had been wafting across east Kolkata ever since. Thousands had been born and died amidst the pestilential rubbish, left to their own devices, ignored, and forgotten. They would still be there when the luxury hotel fad had passed.

The two men stood out like sore thumbs. They were both huge and were continually slapping away at the mosquitoes that were devouring them.

"I hate this fucking country. I hate this shitty city even more. Worse than central Africa. At least there, the women look good and are willing. And this here shithole doesn't feel safe."

Williams, the more phlegmatic of the two men, shrugged into the night. "It's pretty safe. Yes, those kids keep passing us, but they are small fry. But our guy, Dead King, is seriously late."

Mathew cut in. "And what is this, anyway. We hang around for hours just to buy a couple of pea shooters on the recommendation of some film makers who want our money? Let's just give up on the guns, go to a sports store, and buy some baseball bats.

We're not here to rob a bank. We're here to extract a couple of spoilt runaway kids on drugs. How hard can it be?"

"It's cricket, Mathews. They don't know the first thing about baseball in these parts."

One of the young boys who'd been watching the two British men peeled away from a cigarette stall across the road. As he dropped away into a narrow alley leading into the vast landfill, he turned and waved for them to follow.

Williams pushed himself off the wall he'd been leaning against.

"It's no longer about the client back home. There's talk of lost loot. One of the kids we're supposed to repatriate knows where Mother Teresa's money is hidden. We're well placed to be exploiting that, I'd say. Better than anyone else."

Mathews' face lit up. "Now we're talking. Let's go and set the world on fire."

———

Aubrey Bilham-Rolls looked dreadful. The aura he'd gathered within and around himself when he spoke at the mansion had dissipated. His gaunt face, glistening under a film of sour sweat, screamed withdrawal.

Becker and Madhurima found him in his flophouse in Shobhabazar as he was searching his cell-like room for drugs. He wasn't having any luck. Becker stepped into the tiny chamber.

"Aubrey, it's time to go home."

Firangi Baba looked at the two intruders uncertainly. "Can you get me a little opium, guys?"

Madhurima had a little pity in her eyes. Just a little.

"Mr. Bilham-Rolls, you have caused enough mischief with your visions. One man has died. Your brother is missing. It's time to tell your devotees that there is no treasure and then leave the country. Either way, we have tickets for you and your brother to fly home later night. Your father will reimburse the fare."

Firangi Baba nodded. "I will do it tonight. I will go back to the mansion and talk to the people. One last time. If you find my brother. And a little opium."

Madhurima turned to Becker.

"Let's go then."

The short walk to the banks of the Hooghly was excruciatingly slow. Firangi Baba was dragging his feet. He bought cigarettes and chain-smoked all the way to the broken mansion.

They led him to the top of the stairs. His devotees were beginning to gather as the sun dropped into the low Howrah skyline across the river.

"Brothers and sisters, who among you might have a little fin for me. Tonight, I will tell you everything I know. But I need a little help."

Despite his pitiful state, Firangi Baba still impressed his followers, perhaps because he was starting to look like them a little more every day. A faceless, tired addict peeled out of the crowd, pushing a slip of tinfoil ahead of him. There would be no chillum tonight. The junkie spoke no English and simply handed Firangi Baba the foil and a hollow plastic tube. The young sick sadhu invited the man to light his smoke.

Madhurima looked sad and a little angry, but she didn't say anything. As the addict was about to light the foil, a shout sounded across the mansion's courtyard.

"Stop. Stop. No one but me lights my brother's smoke. Get back."

Magnus was limping up the stairs. Becker was shocked to see the young man in an even worse state than his brother. He could smell him before he reached the top stair and pulled a small package from his pants.

"Don't worry, Aubrey, I got the good stuff for you. In a minute, you'll be fine."

He grabbed the foil off the addict and quickly prepared a hit for Firangi Baba. The crowd jostled impatiently below them. Madhurima was on her phone, calling for discreet back-up.

Firangi Baba inhaled deeply and held his breath. Time stood still.

Madhurima stepped up to Magnus. "Who kidnapped you?"

"Dead King from Dhapa."

Madhurima raised her eyebrows.

"That man only kidnaps if he's paid. Who paid to have you kidnapped?"

Magnus pointed down into the crowd. "Our two filmie friends, Gaurav and Roni. They asked this guy, Dead King. Only they didn't pay. That's why I'm back."

Becker scanned the crowd but he couldn't see the film makers. Magnus turned to him.

"Dead King will come after you next."

"Why would he do that?" Becker countered. "I don't know this guy. How would he know me?"

"Gaurav told him. Otherwise his gang of goondas wouldn't have let him go. Gaurav told him that you were here to take us home. That you were working with the cops. He must have seen you with the inspector lady, after Raju was killed. Or maybe Raju's killer saw you two together. They tortured Gaurav. He probably told them anything that came into his head."

Madhurima looked at Becker impassively.

"Kolkata doesn't want you today, Becker. It's time you left and removed this mess from our city."

"I didn't put it here."

"I know," she said, her voice softening.

Firangi Baba got up, fortified by his smoke. He swayed in front of the crowd. Becker felt a shiver run down his back. In the dim evening light, the young man looked impressive despite himself.

"Brothers and sisters," he spread his arms and fell to his knees.

"Brothers and sisters," Firangi Baba tried again, brushing dreadlocks from his sickly face.

His eyes rolled back. The crowd groaned. Madhurima pulled

at Becker's shirtsleeve. He shook his head. If they stopped him now, there'd be a riot. Firangi Baba began to shake. First it looked as if he was cranking up his own motor with theatrics, but his convulsions took on a life of their own. Magnus stepped up and put his arms around him, but the young sadhu wriggled his shoulders out of the embrace, contorting his arms to be free.

"Brothers and sisters, Mother Teresa left us her fortune. I can see it so clearly. She was a clever, wicked woman. She took from the rich. But she cared nothing for the poor. She sent some of her money to the Vatican. She buried some of the money..."

The crowd hung on to his every word. Only the city's never-tiring car horns sounded off far away. A dog barked mournfully. Becker thought it almost comical. But the crowd was hyped up. This time, Firangi Baba had to come up with something. The young sadhu was breathing quickly now, his eyes nowhere, his hands gesticulating as if emphasizing moments in a heated conversation. Even Madhurima looked impressed.

"South Park Cemetery."

Three words. His devotees were on their feet, pushing into an ever tighter semi-circle around the young man. Becker knew the cemetery. It held more than 1600 graves. Unless Firangi Baba uttered something a little more specific, his devotees would likely tear him and the cemetery to pieces. Eternal love and bottomless anger had never been so close.

"Brothers and sister, let's all go. I will show you where our treasure is hidden."

Becker and Madhurima looked at each other.

"He's committing suicide," she whispered.

Firangi Baba snapped out of his trance and rose surprisingly quickly. He spread his arms once more, mimicking a heartfelt embrace, and stalked off into the night. His congregation rushed off in his footsteps as one.

"I just had a call from one of my colleagues who works out in Dhapa. Two male foreigners have been found dead in the landfill Magnus claims to have been held in. No IDs of any kind. But they look like ex-military. Contractors perhaps. We're checking the city's better hotels. Could they be the people you mentioned coming in your wake to rescue the boys?"

Becker was annoyed.

"I will call my client."

Twenty minutes later, they were standing at the entrance to the South Park Cemetery. The road was called Mother Teresa Sarani but had started life as Burial Ground Road. The irony wasn't lost on Becker. The cemetery was locked at night, but Firangi Baba and his brother had found a way in. A van filled with sepoys pulled up. Devotees and hangers-on trickled by and were turned back from the gate by a couple of elderly security guards armed with tired looking bamboo sticks. The rumor mill was doing overtime and Teresa's treasure was now on every-one's lips. The mood among the crowd was ugly. More police were on the way. Becker left the melee and crossed the road.

"Mr. Bilham-Rolls. Good afternoon... Yes, I have found your sons. They're not willing to leave so far, but I am working on that... On another note, did you send anyone else to sort this out... Private contractors?... That was a mistake, and not part of our agreement... No, Mr. Bilham-Rolls, you can't do that...and I don't work for clients who bring competition into the same job... No Mr. Bilham-Rolls, I haven't seen them. But police have... No, they have not been arrested, they're dead, both of them, and your sons may yet go the same way if things here become more inflamed... No, that wasn't the deal, which in any case you have forfeited, bringing in mercenaries..."

He hung up. It felt good to be unemployed. Bilham-Rolls had paid a generous advance. Becker's sense of obligation had shifted to the two boys. And to Madhurima. He returned to the cemetery gates. She was waiting for him.

"Let's go inside."

Becker watched Madhurima check her gun. She was flanked by two armed sub-inspectors. They nodded at Becker curtly.

"Did your client send those mercenaries?"

"He did."

"He didn't trust you to do your job, Becker."

"He didn't, no."

"Are you doing your job?"

He smiled without feeling good. He couldn't quite read her tone of voice.

"With your help, I hope so."

"I hope so too, Becker."

They looked at each other quickly then, and he sensed an immense sadness in her. But it was gone as quickly as it had appeared.

"In more than twenty years of service, I've never shot anyone, Becker. We don't do that much in Kolkata. And I've been lucky. But the city is changing. And not for the better."

Rows upon rows of gothic tombs and mausoleums rose into the night sky as they stepped inside the cemetery. Colonial administrators, judges, scientists, as well as cattle-breeders and jail-keepers lay buried here. As they proceeded into the darkness, the city noise receded, and the ghosts of the past were closing in.

"My men have created a cordon around the entire complex. No one gets in, no one comes out. A pan vendor saw up to ten men, including two foreigners break in earlier."

"And there's only four of us?"

Madhurima smiled. "My colleagues Abishek and Shaquib from Lalbazar Headquarters are among the force's best sharpshooters. They work in extremely stressful situations. They will have our backs. I don't imagine we will encounter heavily armed resistance."

A bat fluttered in front of Becker's face in the near darkness, when he heard a voice. Madhurima had heard it too. The three cops stopped in their tracks. They could make out the cold shine of a mobile phone screen behind a huge Indo-Saracenic tomb to their right. They would have to leave the main path and head amidst the dead, which offered little protection from surprise attacks. Abishek and Shaquib moved ahead silently through knee-high dry grass. Becker formed the rear. He wasn't complaining. As they rounded a huge plinth, an extraordinary scene emerged among pillars and trees in a clearing ahead.

"You will tell me which tomb to dig up or you will hang."

A tough youth, dressed in a longi and a maroon western-style shirt, buttoned up to the neck, his head half-shaved in what probably passed for contemporary, landless hipster fashion, stood surrounded by four other tough guys, facing off Firangi Baba. The young Sadhu had a rope around his neck, which had been slung over the thick branch of a mango tree. Three smart phones lit the scene. A fourth one was filming the strange tableau.

"If you hang me, you'll never find out."

"If you die, I will believe you told the truth about the money. If you live, you must have lied. This is my test for you, foreigner."

The young tough laughed maniacally and took a swig on a bottle of Old Monk rum.

Abishek and Shaquib had drawn their guns and cowered in the dead grass. Becker and Madhurima followed suit. The two sharpshooters shook their heads. They were too far away to use their hand guns.

The rope around Firangi Baba's neck was taut. His bare feet rested on a flimsy plastic stool. But the young man didn't seem all that fazed.

"Becker will be here any second. With the cops."

The young goonda snorted derisively.

"Becker and his friend are dead. They came to us to buy guns. Said they were former British elite soldiers only. We got them to pay for the weapons, and then we shot them with their new weapons. That's what happens in Dhapa when idiots walk in. They are in the landfill. We didn't hide them well, so the police find them soon."

Firangi Baba shook his head frantically in the noose. "Becker doesn't have a friend. He is alone. You got the wrong guys. I don't understand why they call you Dead King. You're an idiot."

The young goonda lunged forward and tapped the plastic stool with his foot. Firangi Baba swayed for his life.

"The Britisher is trying to get himself killed," Madhurima whispered. Becker had to admit that Aubrey's strategy was questionable. He heard a noise behind them and pushed Madhurima into the grass. The two shooters had heard it too and lay perfectly still.

"There they are. Look at that madharchod. He's going to hang a foreigner in the Britisher's cemetery. That's what I call funny."

Gaurav and Roni, the film makers, hustled past them, with Magnus in tow, oblivious to the prone figures in the grass. Roni was carrying a tripod.

"Hey, Dead King. The park is surrounded by cops. They are probably hiding behind every gravestone. It's over, man. Let this guy go. They are already going to fry you bastards for the killing of those two Britishers we sent your way."

Becker smiled as he raised his head slightly. Everyone who mattered was present. No one could be called innocent. Now it was just a question of weeding out the guilty from the semi-guilty.

Dead King dropped his bottle and flicked a short, vicious-looking knife open in his hand and turned towards the new arrivals.

"What are you pieces of shit doing here? I told you I would sort this out."

Gaurav laughed. "And run away to Bihar with Teresa's loot? Fat chance of that."

"There's no loot. This madharchod made it all up. That's why he is going to hang tonight only. He will die. And we will go back to Dhapa. And you two will go to jail. Where you will be raped by men like me. They will be waiting for you. You fucked with Dead King."

Magnus stepped up to his brother and tried to loosen the noose. Dead King waved his knife. "I didn't cut you the first time. But I will do so now if you try and save Firangi Baba. This is not a night for saving. Now tell me where the fucking money is, madharchod. Tell me the truth."

Firangi Baba laughed in the young goonda's face. "Never let the truth get in the way of a good story, man."

The sound of his hysteria echoed between the tombstones. If the dead could hear, they were all listening now.

Gaurav laughed too.

"It's great getting you idiots doing our dirty work. No one will ever know I hired you to kidnap this guy," he said pointing at Magnus. "You are finished. Your friends are finished. Landfill scum doesn't stand a chance in court. No one will believe a word you say. I will talk, and I will walk, and you will hang for the murder of two British tourists. And maybe even a third one," he grinned looking up at Firangi Baba.

"India's for Indians," he added with menace. Becker had the impression that the man excluded the two foreigners and the Dead King's slum dwellers from his vision of what India should be.

The young goonda ignored Gaurav.

"Keep your Hindu nationalist shit to yourself. We're all brothers."

"Because you are all nothing. Because you will never be anything. Even if this foreigner knows where the treasure is, you guys are too stupid to beat it out of him."

"That's right, madharchod," Dead King answered and sauntered right up to Firangi Baba. Without hesitation, he kicked the plastic stool again, playfully. A little too playfully. Firangi Baba lost his balance. Magnus lurched forward and tried to catch his brother's fall. Madhurima rose. Abishek and Shaquib were already running towards the make-shift gallows. The goondas switched their phone torches off as one. The cemetery plunged into darkness. A shot rang out. Another. Seconds later Madhurima switched on a powerful torch. The scene in front of them was pitiful. Firangi Baba dangled from the rope, his feet twenty centimeters off the ground. His brother, at his feet, had failed to stop his fall. Dead King lay in the grass in front of the hanged sadhu. His maroon shirt was leaking blood. His companions had disappeared. Gaurav and Roni stood frozen; their camera trained on the hanging. Becker swallowed hard. He could sense the ghosts all around them, furious at the disturbance.

Madhurima knelt next to Dead King. The young man was dying. A solitary tear rolled down his cheek.

"Madharchod. We never had a chance. Those filmie guys played us. False promises. We never should have left the landfill. Never should have left Dhapa. Out here we die like dogs."

"Gaurav and Roni hired you…?"

Dead King smiled beatifically. "Yes, Teresa's treasure. They wanted to make sure to get it. We kidnapped the brother. We killed the Britishers…they asked us to clean up…no matter. I am prince of Dhapa."

More lights flashed on. Seconds later the clearing was crawling with sepoys. Shaquib sat in the grass, shocked. He'd fired the two shots that had killed the kid from the slums.

"Those whom the gods love die young," he mumbled.

Becker, suddenly angry, shot back. "Right. Only the gods love those poor bastards. No one else in this city does."

Without another word, he went over to Magnus who lay crumpled on the wet grass. His brother had been cut down and was waiting for a body bag. Becker felt disgusted.

"You have a flight to catch tonight. I suggest you cooperate with the cops. I imagine after they have interviewed you, they will be keen to get rid of you. I will take you home to your father."

Madhurima was behind him then. He could sense it without turning. A tsunami of conflicting emotions shot through him. He had always hated cops. He had missed this girl, now a woman, for twenty years. Fate wasn't on their side. Nothing was on their side, not even Kolkata.

"What were these kids thinking, making up a story of Teresa's money?"

Becker sighed without turning. "I think they were trying to become internet sadhus. The worst of both worlds —religion and social media. They needed something to pull in the punters. But they didn't figure that the smell of money, however faint, really just a bullshit story cooked up by a couple of junkies, would catch on with the wrong people so quickly. Naivety and greed killed Aubrey."

She didn't say anything for a long time. Then her phone beeped, and he heard her rise. "We meet under dark stars, Becker. It's the life we chose. You protect your countrymen when they fail to behave like human beings abroad. I protect my city. Calcutta is dead. It's Kolkata now. Remember that and keep it in your heart, Becker."

———

Shaquib accompanied Becker and Magnus Bilham-Rolls to the airport. The British ambassador, a man Becker had been friends with at university, had been in touch, immigration had been informed, the journey home was inevitable. Becker stared numbly out of the window. New high-rises were shooting out of the dusty wasteland on the city's outskirts. But they didn't convey a new beginning. The horror continued unabated along these rising concrete canyons, and millions would be squashed and rubbed out into obscurity between them. Dead King, people like Firangi Baba's devotees, those people on the vague frontiers, those people one never saw, never heard of and never knew about, could be wiped off the face of the earth without people a few hundred meters away even knowing about it. Becker wanted it all to end. Shaquib's phone rang. He handed it to Becker.

"Hello Becker."

"Hello Madhu."

Neither of them spoke as the distance between them increased steadily. Finally, she cleared her throat.

"The film makers set all this in motion. They really thought there might be loot, that Firangi Baba's visions were real. They were never going to work with the foreigners, YouTube channels and all that. They have huge debts from a previous film project. So, they thought kidnapping was the next best thing. They used the kids from Dhapa, knowing full well that if it all went bad, those poor bastards would be blamed. But not this time, Becker. We have everything on tape. They will go down. Dead King is guilty of many crimes. But I agree with you. It's the system that has let him and his friends and family down. We must do better."

Becker swallowed his anger.

"I know how you feel, Becker. And I am so sorry we couldn't reconnect. But I have a family; Emran, my husband, and Devi. And you have your freedom. We must make the most of it."

He didn't answer. The airport loomed up ahead.

"We will always have Calcutta, Becker. That's the best that can be said."

He had to admit it: men were hard, but women were strong.

"Thanks for getting me out of there so quickly. Magnus will be collected when we land in London. My mission won't be accomplished, but it will be over. It was a real pleasure to meet Devi. Make the most of your family. Remain the great cop that you are. Above the fray, full of pride and courage."

He realized he was starting to waffle and stopped.

"Thank you, Becker. You're a great man. Take care."

"If you ever need my help, you know…"

The connection cut. He was alone.

PART THREE

KILLKATA 2039

MEENA AND JOY stood facing each other on stage. The afternoon threw a golden hue on them and gave them a sense of permanence, at odds with the chaos of the drowning city around them. They looked impressive: Meena in her skimpy bikini, her skin light in tone and covered in tattoos; Joy, huge, her breasts bulging under a long black kurta, golden thread running its length. There was an audience of five, all family, not counting a lone langur, on the raised, rickety turnstiles that loomed out of the shallow water that had been covering the Maidan for weeks. It was just a little too deep to wade, so punters arrived in crude wooden rowboats, piloted by Bihari migrants who'd once driven or pulled rickshaws. Beyond the Maidan, the vulgar fingers of two abandoned Trump Towers reached out of the shallow water along Chowringhee. The rest of the city was just as inundated — the water was a little deeper around College Street, with several alleged crocodile sightings. Only Black Town and Salt Lake further north and some of the eastern districts remained dry. But no one ever talked about the eastern districts since Hindu fanatics had built huge camps there to intern their Muslim compatriots. People from central Kolkata never ventured to Dhapa, Topsia, or Tangra, the city's erstwhile

Chinatown. One could never be sure whether one would make it back.

Joy pulled her beard straight, trying to impress her sister with calm authority, but Meena wasn't having it. They'd both been here before. They'd fought and argued and bitched since they'd taken control of the family. Since mama and papa had finally died of their chemical injuries. But today's confrontation was shaping up as the mother of all battles. The little legless ones, Roni and Vicky, also known as the kathi rolls; Rishi, the boy who was old; Behan, the half-wallah; and Tagore, the pyromaniac dwarf; were all up for another screaming match between their older siblings. Perhaps they saw the sisters' feuds as a kind of parenting, since their parents had perished six months earlier, after years of suffering while creating the brood. Everything was a trauma in these trying, dying days.

Meena defiantly stared her sister down.

"Look, the audience comes because of me. I claim fifty percent of the resources. It's only fair. They come to see the all-in-one girl with the cock and pussy. Bearded ladies you can find on every street corner from here to Islamabad. Pay me my share or suffer the consequences."

Joy laughed like Genghis Khan. She looked at her younger sister triumphantly, menace in her huge black eyes. It was the last thing Meena saw.

Everything went dark.

Someone had crept up from behind, pulled a rough cotton sack over her head and swept her off her feet.

She heard Joy's voice from far away. "Mama and Papa always wanted me to lead the brood. This is what you get for challenging the universe, sister Meena. Like a Kali idol, you'll be adored and then you'll be immersed in our holy river. We will take a little bit of a hit in audience numbers, I concede that. But given the peace of mind I will find in return, it's small price to pay. The Little Ones always support the strongest one of us, no matter what. Should've watched your back. Good-bye."

The sack was tied, and Meena felt herself roughly lifted up and slung across a giant's shoulder. She sensed it was Ajinder, the doorman at the Grand Hotel. She'd seen him around their camp in the compound of the Kolkata Police Club, which was almost dry, thanks to the sandbags the cops had amassed there before quitting. Ajinder was not as bad as some, but Meena was sure Joy was paying him handsomely in resources. That's what it was all about in these days of slow submersion. And that's what she'd become. A resource. Woodlands, the last functioning hospital, dry for now in a high-rise in Topsia, was screaming for organs. The camp inmates in the region were dying like flies and — fed on rat meat and moldy rice — were too unhealthy to be of any use. Meena had no illusions about what Joy had meant when she'd spoken about adoration and immersion. They fattened you up on drips loaded with glucose and vitamins before harvesting your kidneys. In a city where nothing worked, organs for the rich continued to be a highly sought-after resource. Meena had heard that some of the Kali Yug gang members had killed each other to sell kidneys. The higher the water rose, the crazier Kolkata got. The only hope one could muster was to survive another day.

———

Becker woke abruptly. Disoriented, he grabbed the water sack by his bedside. His nekphone was vibrating. He'd meant to flick it off before going to sleep. Must have forgotten. One forgot things at sixty-five. His eyes barely open, he quickly scanned the incoming caller info that appeared on his retina. He hated seeing the screen filter between himself and the real world, but without a nekphone one couldn't do anything in this world.

"Yes, who's this?"

No image appeared. The line collapsed and reassembled in digital crack fashion. Even at 3am, the internet was groaning.

The call came from Edinburgh. He was surprised someone still had access to the net up there.

"Hallo, is that you, Becker?"

He knew that voice from of a thousand, a million voices.

"Hi Madhu, yes, it's me. How are you? What a surprise."

He felt a little breathless.

"Becker, it's Devi, Madhu's daughter. Remember me?"

Of course, the woman's voice was young. Well, around 40 anyway. Had it been that long?

"Good morning, Devi. You're in Scotland?"

"Becker, I am sorry to get in touch with bad news. I'm in Scotland and safe for the moment. But my mom, she's no longer safe. She needs help."

He sat up properly and shook his head, pushing the skin around his cheap phone device into a more comfortable position.

"She's in Kolkata?"

"Yes, Becker."

"Kolkata is flooded, Devi. Has been for a year or more."

"I know, Becker... But she wouldn't leave. And now there are no plane tickets. They're no longer sold. The last regular flight out of Kolkata left a month ago. Since then it's been charters, a couple of government specials. Even getting to Delhi isn't easy. The trains are suspended, and the Ganga is so crowded with makeshift boats, that mobility is getting more and more restricted. West Bengal will soon be cut off from the rest of the world."

"Where does that leave Madhurima?"

"She needs to get out. The police force has collapsed. Cops are being hunted across the city's rooftops. By goondas, by those fanatic Kali Yug nationalists. Some Muslims are fighting back, but they're not well organized. It's bad, Becker."

"Wasn't your dad a cop too? Is there nothing he can do?"

"Becker, my father is a Muslim. He was fired years ago when they brought in all those anti-Muslim laws. No one knows where he is. We haven't had any contact for months. It's possible he's been kidnapped. Or he's in a camp. Mum waited and waited. She needs out. You're our last hope."

"Devi, do you know how old I am? I am retired. I'm a pensioner. Or I would be, if the government still paid pensions to former Asia consultants. I don't careen round the world anymore. I haven't been to India in a decade. I'm happy if I get to the toilet and back in one piece nowadays. We had our time. Now we're just waiting to drown..."

"Becker, mum loved you. All her life. She couldn't express it only. You know, convention, morality. And then she had to take care of the family. But I think it's never too late. Sometimes she joked that I was your child, not papa's."

Becker chuckled. "She said that to me once too. But it's not possible."

After he'd clicked off his nekphone, Becker sat on his bed for a long time, listening to the rain that fell incessantly onto the roof of his tiny Bethnal Green studio flat. He tried to remember Madhurima's face, but it didn't quite come into focus. He didn't have a photo of her. Devi's call had profoundly unsettled him. Something in her story didn't add up, but he couldn't put his finger on it.

An hour later he'd called in his last favor from the last British high commissioner and English ambassador to India, Sir Henry Benn. They'd studied together and had both briefly looked into a sordid criminal case in Kolkata twenty years earlier. One ticket on several charter and military planes to Kolkata, two tickets back three days later. The old diplomat had told Becker not to bother to get an Indian visa. Immigration services in the West Bengal capital had collapsed weeks earlier.

"And be careful. The last reports we've had from thereabouts suggested that marauding Hindu death squads are terrorizing villages and towns across West Bengal. Kolkata is under siege and the Muslim-communist resistance is in disarray, like everything else out there. Get in, find your lady friend, keep your head down, and don't miss that last flight. There might never be another. Not one you'd get on anyway. If it were business, I wouldn't help you. But as it's love...there's so little left of that now."

Merely listening to the former ambassador's warning made Becker feel tired, but he packed a bag and headed to Luton Airport, which handled the few international flights connecting England to the rest of the world.

The auto-piloted Boeing 797 Tesla took him as far as Islamabad. The other passengers were all military types, a couple of mid-tier management guys, and a lackadaisical gang of army grunts. Becker had flown the route many times. The sight below them was both exhilarating and frightening. The Hindu Kush had turned a soft green. Huge landslides scarred the mountain ridges and appeared to have subsumed entire valleys. The land around the Pakistani capital looked like soft mud.

As soon as they touched down, the English disappeared into a fleet of waiting SUVs. The plane was back in the air minutes later. Becker's next flight was eight hours away, a missionary plane heading into Delhi. He didn't dare leave the airport, almost pitch dark as it was. There was no staff, the only restaurant was closed. His nekphone wasn't working. He was hot, sitting by the edge of the run-way, outside one of the locked departure gates. The entire terminal was subsumed by marijuana plants. Nature was making a come-back, untrammeled by human interference. During the long night, shadows shifted across the runway. Groups of hungry-looking men sharing hand-rolled cigarettes, looking for a way out where there was none, drifted by. If they saw him, they left him alone. The white man no longer had anything to offer. The rising waters offered the same immeasurable cruelty to the Netherlands as to Karachi. At the end of times, we were all equal, he mused, glad that whoever was out there didn't beat him to death out of boredom. At dawn, an old man emerged from somewhere in the main terminal with a flask of hot tea.

"As-salāmu ʿalaykum. I used to work here. I have no family. Will you share tea with me?"

"Wa ʿalaykumu s-salām," Becker replied, happy to have company.

They sat side-by-side in silence. The tea, if that's what it was, was sickly sweet. Imran asked Becker if he could get him out. Becker didn't answer. What was out?

When the sun finally showed up, the Christians did too. They wheeled a small plane out of a hangar — an ancient 20-seater Yadav, made in India and never known for its reliability. Becker sighed inwardly as he showed his ticket to the suspicious pilot. He waved tiredly at Imran and climbed aboard. Dying in a plane crash was probably better than being marooned on the Islamabad runway.

As they swept into the rising sun and flew east, Becker felt like he could watch the transformation of the planet. Lahore was being whipped by a sandstorm that rattled the flimsy Yadav and made Becker feel like the bag of old bones he was. The man next to him began to pray before reaching for the sick bag. There wasn't one. Jesus had left on an earlier flight, along with all the other gods that anyone had ever prayed to, probably to Mars. What was left, was bleak. The dust storm continued all the way into the Indian capital. Delhi was infernally hot. Narendra Modi International Airport was still open for business, for those with the means. Armed troops milled around thousands of passengers, most of them affluent, entitled, and stressed to breaking point. A couple of 797 Teslas stood on the melting tarmac, disorderly queues of exhausted, fighting people stretching back to the departure gate. Becker knew that one of the huge auto-piloted beasts was bound for Kolkata. Most of the would-be passengers on the runway were waiting for flights west. He would be among them in a few days' time.

Madhurima woke with a start. She'd dreamt of Emran. She'd seen him floating in a pond in Ballygunge, one she'd passed many times when she was young. She checked her nekphone and sunk back onto the mattress. There was nothing. Nothing except the smell of damp, the sound of water trickling from one place to another. As she sank back into exhaustion, her nekphone vibrated. Her interface had long broken down. Only the audio was working.

"We have your husband Emran. Give us resources or we will hand him over to the Kali Yug gangs. And be quick, as they already know that we have him. They've made an offer. One international flight, to Europe or the US, that's your fee. Otherwise we'll behead your husband for the crazies. I call back tomorrow only."

"How do I know you really have him?"

"How do you think I got your number, madharchod?"

"I want to talk to my husband. Let me talk to him and I will get you the resource."

The line went dead. Madhurima inhaled deeply in the dark and reached for the light switch. She sat up in shock. A life sign. She hadn't heard from Emran for months. She didn't have anything to bargain with. She certainly didn't have any airline tickets. No one could get those. But she had to find a way. She had to save Emran. She owed him. A lifetime. Of love, affection, and support. She fretted a moment over having called Becker back into her life. But he was the only other man in the world she could trust. And these were desperate times. Her nekphone vibrated.

"Madhu. Emran here."

"Darling," her voice almost failed her. "I am so glad to hear you voice. It's been months. You are alive."

"I am fine, Madhu. They are treating me well at the Maidan. But time is short. These Kali Yug bastards have already been here and made an offer. Can you get a ticket?"

A thought crossed her mind and was gone before she could answer.

"I will find a way."

She could hear laughter somewhere close to her husband.

"I love you, Madhu. I know I never told you that enough..."

"Emran..."

Her husband was gone, replaced by the earlier caller. A woman's voice, deep and guttural.

"So, listen, you have until tomorrow to set things in motion. We're not monsters, but we need guarantees. You're the wife, so you're our preferred client. But if you don't come up with the resources, we'll sell him to the Kali Yug. And you know what they do with elitist, educated Muslims. Any kind of Muslims. They have offered to pay us handsomely to behead your husband in front of an audience of hundreds, maybe thousands, maybe tens of thousands."

The line went dead. Madhurima knew exactly where her husband was. She knew the woman who'd made the demand. Emran's kidnappers were sly, but they were also sloppy, amateur. Her heart almost jumped out of her mouth. Now there was hope. For the first time in months, there was hope. Had she been twenty years younger, she would have paid them a visit now, simply walked in, shot a couple of people, and walked out with Emran. But she wasn't, and those days of thinking and doing and achieving were past. Now she would have to be sly also.

———

Becker managed to get a cab outside the airport. It was an old, yellow Ambassador that had been battery-fitted, the only one of its kind in the row of banged up vehicles in from of the international terminal. The driver offered to take him just beyond Shobhabazar. After that he would have to find other means to get into town.

The sun was just coming up as they left the airport. The sun wasn't visible of course, but the darkness made way to hot, dirty, milky light. Visibility was limited, no more than a couple of hundred meters. The air was so damp that his cotton shirt stuck to his chest in seconds. Welcome back to Asia.

The driver operated the vehicle manually. Perhaps the car was so old, it didn't have self-drive technology. Becker worried he might die in an accident brought on by human error. He hadn't been in a car driven by a person for a decade. But then, back when he was young, he'd driven himself thousands of miles. He sighed staring at the relentless wall of concrete blocks covered in tattered digital ad hoardings, most of which produced white noise or nothing at all, from the airport past Rajarhat and into North Kolkata. Laketown lived up to its name. Water began to cover the road in a solid, filthy, shallow film. A few minutes later, Becker stood on what had been Girish Park Road, now a canal of sorts. Those who needed to travel could choose between rickety, wooden, row boats, operated for the most part by wizened old men who looked like their time was almost up, or slightly snazzier vessels with small, noisy outboard motors that were being revved furiously by young street punks to attract passengers. The Indian penchant for improvisation, jugaad, lived on in Kolkata.

"Resources, resources," the drivers shouted when Becker tried to offer a few hundred rupees to one of the motorized water taxis. The third one he tried took his money. It wasn't the return he'd imagined. But then Becker had never expected to return to Kolkata at all. He was looking at ancient history. And that's what he got, all the way down Central Avenue past the Statesman building, now a paramilitary post, sandbagged three meters high, and the blackened shell of the Tipu Sultan Mosque. They passed bloating corpses, dogs for the most part, and a couple of women, their brightly colored saris trailing behind them like blood, before they floated onto Chowringhee. Sitting in a leaking boat, gliding across pestilential water wasn't what he'd envisioned. India had always been a land of surprise and excess. And Kolkata had always been a city either rising or falling, or both.

The Grand Hotel, known as the Oberoi until the city's collapse, was the only accommodation that still took online bookings. Perhaps it just stayed open out of pride. When he'd messaged, the management had informed him only the rooms on the upper floors were available and that he'd have to find his own vessel to reach the hotel. Tucked away amongst flooded, empty shops on Chowringhee, the hotel's drive was under water. A giant Sikh with a drooping moustache and a damp turban, standing on a sagging collection of sandbags, opened the door for him. The floor in the lobby was wet. Instead of a luggage cart, a small dingy, pulled by a member of staff in wellies propelled his bag towards the sole elevator in working order. They'd given him Room 301, a suite with three balconies overlooking the hotel's inner courtyard, which had once held a pool but was now a placid expanse of dark green water. The TV no longer worked, but the internet was still running. As soon as he'd caught his breath, Becker scanned his nekphone for messages. Madhu's face flickered across his retina, fuller, older, with some deep lines where there'd been youth and middle-age, but just as determined as he remembered her, luminous. He remembered then how she'd always been a presence in his life. He'd never married. He'd told himself all his life that he wanted to remain free. He'd never figured out whether that had been an excuse to refrain from pursuing her or whether she'd been an excuse to remain alone. Thanks to the nekphone he could see her when he closed his eyes and let himself float away.

"Becker. You are here."

"I am."

He looked at her for a long while. Emotions washed over him, the way the rising sea washed into the city.

"You can see me, but I can't see you, Becker. My nekphone is playing up. I hate these things. I will be at the Grand in an hour. I want to see what you look like. I am so happy you came."

She hung up. He started to sweat even though the suite was cool. An hour. It had been twenty years. And twenty years before that. What strange lives people led. There wouldn't be another twenty, of that he was sure. And what did he look like? The mirror in the bathroom was fading, but so was the man staring into it. He was still staring when reception rang his nekphone. Madhu had arrived. She was on her way up.

Something felt wrong, when everything should be going according to plan.

———

Meena stared across at Ajinder. They were in a tiny staff room in the Grand Hotel. She heard water dripping. The walls were covered in furry mold and the smell of damp was almost as bad as the air inside the sack she'd been in for the past hour.

"Joy told me to take you to Topsia and hand you over to Woodlands. We have till tomorrow to figure out how to pay her."

The huge sadar smiled at her.

"Unless you can help me out. Like I've helped you out."

"Why do you work for Joy? She's pure bastard. She should never lead the brood. She's using everyone to get more resources. Greedy she is."

"Is it real?"

"Well, you've seen the show."

"You have?"

"Yes, I have a penis, but I am a girl. With a vagina. I'm double trouble. It's not just my stage name. Since birth. You know the story. The Reliance chemical spill, my parents exposed. After Joy was born with hair all over, they got to thinking. Produced six more of us in quick succession. We're all as untouchable as they come. In fact, we're all beautiful," she was searching for words, but pulled off her shirt instead, showing off her three small breasts, covered in lotus flower tattoos, "and ugly."

Ajinder looked away.

"My little brother, Pavan. The Kali Jug think he's a Muslim. Joy's got him stashed away somewhere. Threatening to sell him to those monsters if I don't do her dirty work. He's only twelve."

"What sort of dirty work?"

"I kidnapped you."

"Apart from that. What else did you do for her?"

Ajinder refused to meet her eye.

"You must understand. I'm in a difficult situation."

It was barely a question, and she had problems squeezing the words from her throat.

"You killed them when Joy turned sixteen, didn't you? You killed my parents?"

Ajinder nodded, tired.

"I killed them. I mean, they were almost dead. They were suffering."

"That never got in the way of their plans," Meena mused bitterly. "Some parents."

Ajinder nodded.

"So, what now? You're a big man. You could crush her in an instant."

"And lose my brother forever. She says he's still alive."

"But you don't know that. I've never heard about Joy holding a kid prisoner somewhere."

Ajinder looked crestfallen.

"Sorry."

Meena was pretty sure that the Sikh's brother was dead. A twelve-year-old with healthy organs fetched a high price in Kolkata.

"Did you ever ask to speak to your brother? A nekphone call would prove he's alive."

Ajinder shook his head. He was a pretty meek guy for a giant. And he had some humanity. Meena owed him her life. She would repay him if possible. But to do that, she'd have to get rid of Joy, get the family back in line, and think of something better to do than to run a freak show on the Maidan. She was more than her genitals. Her siblings were more than their features, or the lack of them.

"I do know that Joy is holding an ex-cop hostage. High ranking. A Muslim. Used to be a deputy commissioner. She's blackmailing his wife who was once a famous detective. The grandniece of Feluda, can you believe it?"

"The detective from the 1960s? I thought he was a fictional character."

Ajinder shook his head. "I met Feluda once. Long back, when I started at the Oberoi. He was long retired by then and had become an astrologer, a sort of oracle that the city's well to do asked for help when they faced supernatural challenges. He came to look at a haunted room. Found out there was a fresh corpse under the floorboards and guests had been hearing rats and other creepies plucking at it at night. A gruesome tale in those days that never made the papers. I shook his hand."

"So, you know the grand-niece, the woman being blackmailed?"

"Yes, she came into the hotel every now and then, both on- and off-duty. But usually for work. She was a good cop, stayed inspectress all her life. Liked to work the streets. She's in her mid-sixties now. As is her husband. I know them both. I've worked at the Oberoi for twenty years. Started at fourteen."

"So, if we busted out this cop…"

Ajinder grinned with a little more confidence than he'd been able to muster since they'd arrived at the hotel.

"You see, Joy has already sold this man to the Kali Yug. She's collected resources in exchange for conducting a public beheading on the Maidan. Next week apparently. She's trying to squeeze resources out of the wife, an airplane ticket west, apparently. So, if you found a way to free Joy's hostage, the Kali Yug and the perhaps the cop's wife would come for her."

Meena nodded, deep in thought. Things were going to work out.

"Perhaps your brother is alive after all. If Joy keeps this policeman, she is organized enough to have other hostages. And you might ask for proof one day of course and deny services. In fact, you should consider this now. Insist on a life sign. Rattle the cage a bit. Perhaps we can help each other, Ajinder."

The Sikh stared at her, his eyes full of hope and fear. She put her shirt back on.

"Does the Grand Hotel still have a bar?"

––––––

"Hello Becker. It's been a while."

"Twenty years appears to have become our rhythm."

They stood a meter apart. Madhurima was dressed in a beige shalwar kameez, a worn leather handbag across her shoulder. Her headscarf had slipped back to reveal thick graying hair. Becker was in jeans and a white short-sleeve cotton shirt.

"Forever the handsome sahib."

"Forever the wily inspectress."

She burst out laughing. It was a little forced. Just a little. She didn't embrace him. Nor did Becker step forward. The meter between them remained a chasm.

"Thanks. I am so grateful. I tried. My husband disappeared six months ago. I've turned every stone in this city over three times. I've called in every favor. The Kali Yug are after him, but they don't have him. And I am getting sick. There's no clean water, not enough decent food. Unless you're staying at the Grand Hotel. You made a good choice. The Broadway is a den of thieves nowadays."

Becker relaxed. He'd been so tense, but now that she'd said her piece, he was fine. It had been twenty years. She had her reasons for lying to him whatever it was she was lying about. Probably the husband. She was clearly happy to see him and nervous about having reached out to him. It was like it had always been. The distance between them hadn't increased over the decades, it had been there from the start. He waved towards a heavy wooden desk, pulling his travel documents from his overnight bag.

"I have two tickets back to London. It's a couple of long hops, a night on the runway in Islamabad. I also have visa clearance for you for England. Once there, you can make your way to Scotland, to Devi."

She touched his arm as she took a close look at the documents. He leaned into her ever so slightly and she smiled at their conspiracy, and perhaps her own deviance. It was the times, Becker assured himself. Bad enough to turn anyone into a beast. Bad enough to move the last shred of sanctity from one's life. The first casualty of war was the truth, they said. The first casualty of climate change was everything.

"I don't know what to say, Becker. You saved my career once, now you're saving my life. Plane tickets are like gold in Kolkata."

She picked up one of the documents and scanned through it.

"And I won't have any troubles entering England?"

Becker shook his head.

"Nope. Part of the deal. I pulled in a last favor from the former British and then English high commissioner. Actually, you might remember him. He helped get that boy out, Magnus, I think. The last time we saw each other."

"How could I forget, Becker? Mother Teresa's loot. What an incredible case," she answered a little shrilly. Then she pulled herself together. She dropped the ticket back on the table, with only a slight, almost imperceptible hint of reluctance.

"Ok, Becker. Thanks. Again. I will be forever indebted to you. It's confusing me a little. And leaving India… I mean, we both know…"

He cut her off with a gentle wave of his hand. The last of the afternoon sun threw an impossibly adoring light on her.

"It's great to see you, Madhurima. I guess it feels good to have gotten older. I have a good life back in London, or at least I did until things started seriously crumbling. I don't have kids. I never married. I mean, I was in relationships. But it never worked out for a long run. I'm delighted to help out the one woman whose always been a presence, however remote, all through my adult life. And that's all there's to it. Let's go to England. Then we'll see."

For a moment her heart and soul appeared to buy into the dream. She smiled at him with real warmth and shook her head playfully. Becker bathed in this moment of radiance until it had died off and turned to ash.

"I'd like to stay, Becker, but I better wrap up my affairs. See a couple of old friends. Don't worry, I won't tell them a thing about the tickets. In fact, we should perhaps get out of town for a few days and lay low. I will organize a car. You will have to drive. You remember how to drive?" she asked mockingly.

He nodded, more solemnly than he cared to.

"I haven't driven in years. I feel honored that you'd trust me to drive you around the corner, never mind to…?"

"Darjeeling, Becker, I have a house in Darjeeling. You know, where they used to grow the tea. It used to be our summer hide-away. It's a beautiful property outside of town, an old zamindar home on a ridge. It's got its own vegetable garden. I always thought I'd retire there. But I am too old to dig weeds. We should drive up there for a few days. I can still get petrol."

She laughed nervously. "I mean, in a way, we barely know each other. It would be like saying goodbye to my old life and saying hallo to a new one."

Becker looked at her with a non-committal expression. Madhurima was upset. She opened her handbag and dug through its contents. She found a bunch of keys and put them on the table next to the tickets.

"Here are the keys. So, you can be sure it won't be like

twenty years ago. Or forty years ago. This time, as time's running out, we will finally have some time for each other."

He swallowed hard and let it go. It was all too weird. He stared at the keys, trying to figure out why and how he was being bought off.

Madhurima tried for her most sincere smile and it almost worked. She was still there. She was still his as much as she'd ever been. But he sensed she had bigger problems than getting out of Kolkata. Problems she didn't care to share. A pity, and yet he felt relief. He'd come to the end of the world to offer a woman he barely knew — but had always loved — a way out of a drowning world. That was his mission. It was all he had to offer. He shrugged, a sign of age probably, and took an involuntary step back to the desk. The tickets were still there. The keys to her house in the hills lay next to them. There was some symbolism, but Becker didn't care to read too much into it. Acting on his training as a psychological consultant would only lead to disillusion. And there was enough of that going around already. He hadn't come all this way to make Madhurima feel she owed him something.

"How are you getting out of Chowringhee?"

"I have a small boat waiting downstairs. My chowkidar drives it."

"We might need that to go towards the airport."

She nodded weirdly. He let it go. It was time to see if the Grand Hotel still had a bar. Liqueur always told the truth.

"I'll walk you out, Madhu."

It was the first time Becker had called her Madhu in two decades.

———

Meena, short on cash but big on revenge, had been sipping her bottle of ThumsUp for an hour when Ajinder loomed next to her, pointing at an old foreigner with blond-white hair who'd just sat down at the long counter of the Raja Bar underneath a wall of early 20th century prints depicting times that would never return.

"That guy there, his name is Becker. A Britisher. He just met Madhurima Mitra in his suite. Turns out they know each other from way back when she was inspectress. I've heard they even worked together. There can't be more than a handful of foreigners in Kolkata right now, so this guy must be here for a reason. In fact, I reckon he's here to get her out. He arrived today from the airport. I just watched him put her into a boat. They're very familiar with each other. Maybe she asked him to help her spring her husband."

Meena watched the white man unobtrusively for a while. He looked to be in his early sixties. He had one of the older models nekphones fitted. He was drinking a large Kingfisher, probably part of Kolkata's last stash of beer. He looked tired but capable. Meena had never spoken to a foreigner before. She gathered her courage and crossed to the counter, more businesslike than sensual, she thought.

"Buy me a drink, Becker, and I will tell you a story."

The foreigner looked at her in surprise.

"Have we met?"

"I have information for you."

The foreigner shrugged. "I'm not sure I want to know more about what's going on in this city than I already do. How do you know my name? Who are you? What do you want?"

Meena could feel people. She looked at the old man closely. He wasn't upset. He wasn't hostile. He probably thought she was interesting. He looked like he was trying to decide whether she was worth talking to. She threw him her best coquettish smile and as much rope as she dared without the risk of hanging herself.

"I am Meena. I am a performer. I know you have come to see the police lady. I know where her husband is."

The foreigner didn't reply. He looked at her, a little shocked perhaps. At last he turned and waved for the bartender. Meena groaned inwardly. She was going to be thrown out.

"What would you like to drink, Meena? The next one's on me and it doesn't have to be ThumsUp. And you tell me how your so-called information relates to me and what you suggest I do about it."

"I don't know what to drink in here, Becker. I have never been in a bar like this."

A second later she had a mojito in her hands.

"What kind of a performer are you?"

"My family runs a circus on the Maidan. Ever since Kolkata started falling apart. I have sex on stage every night. I have a cock and a pussy. People love me. In the early days, they used to come from all over West Bengal. Now it's just Kolkatans. But my sister Joy had me kidnapped and wanted to sell me to a hospital. She wanted to take over. She did take over. Lucky for me, the man who was supposed to deliver me to my death is my friend."

Becker still looked suitably shocked. He didn't ask any questions.

"My sister, she keeps hostages. Your friend's husband among them. She has already sold him to the Kali Yug. Only a plane ticket will buy him off. And Joy is blackmailing your friend for such a ticket, pretending to be a broker between the gangs and your friend. But I think she won't pay the Kali Yug. She will abandon the Little Ones and use the ticket herself."

This time, Becker looked fully engaged.

"And where would I get a plane ticket from, even if it was in my interest to buy this man out?"

Meena put on her best smile again.

"You have two tickets lying on your desk. Tickets are every-thing in Kolkata, old man. They belong in a safe."

Becker got up. "In that case, Meena, I better go and secure these precious documents, don't you think? Otherwise I'm just asking for trouble."

Meena grabbed the Britisher's arm, a little too hard, and

regretted it immediately. She didn't like the look he gave her as he recoiled.

"My sister tried to have me butchered for my kidneys. My four younger siblings are all severely disabled and will die if no one looks after them. I'm sorry, I touched you like this, Britisher. You don't need to fear me. I want to save my family. You want to help your friend. We can work together."

She saw anguish in his face. He knew what she was. So did she.

"Oh, I fear you, don't you worry about that," the Britisher said quietly and smiled. Meena was impressed. Her first foreigner.

———

Becker left the pale looking man-woman in the bar and headed for his suite. He would have to put the tickets in a safe location, but he wasn't entirely sure where that might be. As he opened the door to 301, he noticed that the lights were on inside. His heart jumped. He didn't know whether to retreat or face his intruder. But the sound of the door opening would have alerted anyone inside anyway. Becker felt himself pulled forward. As he stepped into the lounge, Madhurima whipped around in front of the desk, a gun trained on Becker. Years later it occurred to him that this was probably the most heart-breaking moment in his life. But the cruel world healed almost all wounds eventually. She dropped the gun to her side, pale as a ghost.

"I'm sorry, Becker, I didn't think it would be you."

With some effort, he countered gently. "Who did you expect to enter my room, Madhu?"

She stood there helplessly, and he felt a little ashamed for his sarcastic retort. One of the plane tickets poked out of her handbag.

"There are only these two tickets. You need one to buy him out. That still leaves Joy with nothing, because she has already cashed in resources from the Kali Yug who claim your husband. So, she will want both tickets. That means no one gets out. And even if you get away with one ticket, who will take it? Your husband, whose life is in danger? You, because otherwise you will never see your daughter again? Or me, the owner of the ticket?"

Madhurima slumped into the desk chair. Becker didn't like the way she put the gun on her lap. She looked defeated.

"All my life, I tried to be honest, fair, and loving. Emran was kidnapped months ago. Only just recently did the kidnappers demand resources."

"Before Devi got in touch with me?"

"Yes," she sighed. "I am sorry. I had been thinking about if for months after he'd gone. I was sure they'd killed him. They kill everyone. Then I heard from the kidnappers. I had already made up my mind to ask Devi to contact you. Just like last time. I could see it would turn out to be a train crash, but what was I to do?"

"So, you thought you'd steal these tickets, get him out by whatever means, and disappear? That's why you gave me the keys to your house in Darjeeling?"

She nodded numbly.

"Yes, Becker."

She pulled the tickets out of her bag and laid them back on the desk, next to the keys. As if turning back time.

"Look, this is all so stressful. With your permission and the tickets as bargaining chips, I'd like to try to get Emran out. Otherwise he will be killed. Once he is gone, we head for Darjeeling. The floods will never touch us there. I know some people living up there. The community is pretty functioning. Our time will come, Becker."

She was ashen-faced. He wanted to embrace her. But it wasn't their way.

"Madhu..." he trailed off, trying to make up his mind.

"I am sorry, Becker. We had a sacred bond. I broke it."

"Give me your gun."

She shook her head.

"Madhu, if you trust me, give me your gun. I came five thousand miles to reunite you with your daughter. I'm still determined to do that."

She looked down at her weapon, torn up and full of doubt. He knew her so well. A few days across sixty years, but Becker knew her so well. And he felt, through her, he'd come to know himself.

"Becker, tell me what you'll do. Tell me."

"I'm not going to shoot your husband, Madhu. I'm not going to shoot anyone. And the less an ex-cop knows what I'll do to spring another ex-cop, the better."

She got up, finally. She handed him the gun — a well-kept Glock — reluctantly and pulled a box of ammunition from her bag.

"I don't know what the future will bring. Or if there is a future," she mumbled.

He wanted to grab her then, to tell her everything would be alright, even as he knew it couldn't be. He wondered whether such hollow emotional melancholy would be lost on a pragmatic Indian woman who'd fought crime for forty years.

"We've got two days till the plane goes. Keep your nekphone switched on at all times. I'll be in touch if I succeed."

He felt half-crazy, half-silly, saying this. Like an aged underdog hero in a B-movie from the last millennium.

———

The Little Ones looked awful. Something had bitten Vicky, and his eyelid was swollen shut. Tagore looked half-mad with hunger. Roni was nowhere to be seen. Meena felt a wave of anger cursing through her ice-cold innards as she scanned the dark, damp shack behind their stage. Tonight was the night of revenge. It was all about the timing now. Behan waved weakly from his couch. Joy stood perfectly still, frozen in shock. Meena noticed that her sister had put on weight in the few short days since her kidnapping. No one except the very rich who lived behind high walls or were on the way to the airport, put on weight in Kolkata. Next to Joy, a narrow, hard man wearing a white sleeveless undershirt and a saffron gamcha stared at her in obvious disgust. Kali Yug. Meena was tempted to shoot her sister right then, but instead she moved the gun carefully to Joy's left and shot the gang wallah in the chest. Ajinder who towered right behind her, whistled through his teeth.

Joy cried out. "You've just unleashed hell on us, you stupid cunt. They will eat us alive."

Meena was calm. Keeping the gun trained on her sister, she stepped across to Vicky.

"Where's your brother Roni?"

The Little One refused to meet her eye.

Joy laughed behind her. "We called them kathi rolls for a reason. I ate the little bastard. No worse than eating a cow. Cooked him thoroughly. Strange, but none of the other siblings wanted a taste. So, I gorged myself."

Meena turned to face her sister. For a fraction of a moment, sororicide was on her mind. Then she checked herself. It wasn't all about Meena. It was about more than that. If she was going to survive. If the remaining Little Ones were to survive, she would have to be cunning. Brutal was too easy. Everyone else was in on that.

"Where do you keep your hostages?"

Joy laughed. "You'll kill me if I tell you. You'll free that half-dead brother of Ajinder's. You'll take my other high-value hostage. I'm dead the next day. The Kali Yug may forgive me for having one of theirs killed on my plot. But they won't forgive me for letting this Muslim police wallah go. No deal. Shoot me if you have to. But be quick about it, those thugs will be here soon, looking for their friend. And they will kill all of us if they find him dead."

"I have another high-value hostage. A Britisher. I need to hide him. He will fetch more resources than your shabby ex-cop."

Joy raised her heavy eyebrows. "A compromise? So unlike you, Meena. Why would you trust me?"

"I don't trust you. But I need to hide this firangi until I can sell him."

Joy's face lit up.

"I'll have to charge you some rent of course. Some resources are needed. I have to feed the man. Where is he?"

Meena waved to Ajinder who stepped outside the shack. An instant later he was back, pushing a disheveled Becker, his hands bound, ahead of him. Joy clapped her hands with glee.

"He has two plane tickets stashed away. Our escape," Meena whispered, so the Little Ones couldn't hear it. Joy looked at her sister with new-found respect.

"I always thought you were the more devious of the two of us. Our parents' most perfect creation. But you've blown all expectations to hell, Meena. You're fucking a deviant. Inside and out. We can be friends again."

Joy took a step forward. The Little Ones applauded. But Meena didn't lower her gun and nodded towards the thin blade that had slipped from Joy's doti into her right hand.

"That'll take some time, Joy. But I'm willing to go the extra mile. I won't kill you. And you'll take us to your secret prison, so we can store this Britisher. And then we negotiate. We negotiate with whoever might pay for the hostages. And you and I will negotiate. For our kingdom. And more."

The Little Ones clapped again. Joy appeared to mull her sister's proposition over. Meena was restless. She stepped over to the dead gang wallah without lowering her gun. She could see the outlines of his nekphone.

"Does his gang know where the hostages are?"

Joy nodded sourly.

"Then they are already on the way there. They know this guy is dead. Where they fuck do you keep them?"

"They're on the upper floor of the Marble Palace. But only I know how to get there by boat. They will have to walk the last kilometer through Black Town. We can get there before they do."

Meena nodded at Ajinder who pushed Becker out of the shack onto a narrow ledge of sand bags. She waved her gun at her sister.

"Let's go."

"You're going to kill me."

Meena shook her head emphatically.

"You're my sister. We'll work something out."

The boat ride north was horrendous. At night, the full terror of the city's lawlessness bloomed. Madhu's boat was fast, and Meena was a good pilot, navigating the overloaded vessel through tableaux of extreme violence and loss. The Little Ones were sitting quietly crammed together at the bow. Joy sat between his siblings and Becker, who'd loosened the ties around his hands sufficiently to free himself in seconds. He wasn't sure it was worth it. The destruction was incredible. Raj Bhavan, the governor's residence, was on fire. Meena had told Becker that the building had been smoldering for weeks. The recent break in the rains, in league with a persistent army of arsonists, both enraged and encouraged by the absence of government, who gathered around erstwhile seats of power every night, were bringing down the last vestiges of order. The GPO too was under attack by Kali Yug thugs, so engrossed in their efforts to erase the past that they took no notice of the boat and its strange gaggle of passengers. North of BBD Bagh, Joy directed her sister through a maze of narrow alleys. The water level decreased the further they proceeded. In an alley behind Nakhoda Masjid, the city's largest mosque, Ajinder disembarked to remove a family of six who'd been murdered in front of their house and now served as a dam for the shallow, putrid water that sloshed around the buildings.

Becker knew that London was going the same way. More affluent nations would hold out a little longer before descending into anarchy. But not all that much longer. Scotland had walled off the border. The continent had stopped trading with the English. American ships were becoming intermittent. In the US too, far right anarchy was taking hold. In the American south, hundreds of people shot each other every day. What he saw in Kolkata would repeat itself in every low-lying capital close to the sea.

The Marble Palace loomed out of the darkness ahead. The street lights along the sprawling property had been smashed, but an almost full moon was rising as they disembarked, with Tagore having to carry Behan and Vicky. Joy entered the open gates to the complex first. Becker had freed his hands. He felt his pockets to reassure himself. The tickets, the box of bullets, and the keys were still there. The Glock had been fully loaded when he'd passed it to Meena. She had sixteen shots. He hoped she wouldn't need them. Right now, she was pointing the weapon at the back of Joy's head.

"You Little Ones hide in the bushes by the house. We'll come and get you later. Whatever happens, don't move. "

She shushed Tagore towards low brush that embraced the northern façade of the building and reached up to its Corinthian pillars. The moonlight bathed the building's forecourt in zombie-dead luminosity. Becker knew the building; he'd visited forty years earlier when it had been a museum displaying the gaudy baubles of a zamindar family. They left the Little Ones and rounded the palace, almost up to their waists in the water. There'd been a private zoo in the garden once, but it had been replaced by the pond they waded through.

The grand ballroom was lit with dozens of torches. They could hear voices inside. A guard, dressed in saffron gamcha walked past, carrying a wooden club. Ajinder was up the wet stairs and brutally pulled at the man's legs. The guard crashed chin first onto the marble floor. Ajinder pulled him down the stairs and into the dark water.

Becker wished he had the gun, though he didn't actually know how to use one. He'd never shot anyone. He watched Meena drop the Glock into the pocket of her Shalwar as she pushed Joy into the ballroom. She briefly turned to Becker, suggesting with a nod and a smile he stay put. He stayed put, hanging in the doorway with Ajinder.

A collective roar of surprise welcomed the strange siblings. A dozen or so young, tough men who'd sat cross-legged on the polished marble of the ballroom jumped up as one and grabbed for their weapons. The walls were lined with moldy oil paintings, but most of the antique clutter Becker remembered from his previous visit, a life time ago, had vanished. At the far end of room, a fat, bald man in orange robes had risen from a rickety throne. One of his men handed him a spear. He was the man to talk to. Two men cowered on the ground, their feet bound. Becker heard Ajinder hyperventilating behind him.

"It's Pavan. It's my brother. There, on the floor. We must intervene."

Ajinder tried to push past Becker who pushed back against the giant.

"Not yet. Let Meena do her thing first."

Making sure Ajinder stayed behind him, Becker counted the men in the room carefully. Fourteen unfriendlies, including the head goonda. They had plenty of weapons, though none of them remotely modern. They had no guns. A couple of them had cross bows. Becker had no idea how accurate these things were.

"Namaste, Joy. What brings you and your sister here? You have reunited? Made up? You're not sending her to the organ Dhapa after all? What does that mean? Are we still friends?"

The head goonda's words ricocheted around the ball room.

The torches, the booming voice, the fading grandeur, it was all very theatrical.

Meena stepped forward, though she took care to remain behind her older and larger sister.

"We've come to make a deal. We've come to collect your prisoners."

The head goonda stepped past his prisoners and approached Meena, slowly and carefully, like a cat.

"I am the Big B. You know what that means, little sister? You know what that means to you?"

Becker understood enough Hindi to follow the conversation.

"You're Amitabh Bachhan? I don't think so. He's dead. And he's not a half-naked fanatic. He advertised pens, man. He had class, man. Sixty years ago, he played underdogs like me. You look like someone who would use a pen to clean his asshole only."

Becker couldn't believe it. This wasn't diplomacy.

The Big B laughed. It sounded a little forced. Joy started pleading.

"Meena is joking, Da. She kidnapped me and forced me to bring her here. She has no intention of making a deal. She wants our hostages."

The goonda turned to the bearded lady.

"You brought them here?"

"Yes. She has another hostage. That's what she told me. She wanted to hide him here. But now I think he's not a hostage. She tricked me. My sister tricked me."

The Big B raised his spear a little and rolled his eyes.

"In Benares, we drown ugly low-caste Hindus like you at Manikarnika Ghat. Twenty-four-hour power, no food, no shower. Thousands of them. Shiva can't get enough. You two, we'll drown you in the pond outside."

Joy shook her head, frantically.

"No, no, you have to trust me, I am bringing you a gift. I've got everything you want."

The Big B snorted derisively, and his men laughed.

"My guard, did you love him to sleep?"

Joy started crying. "The sadar's brother killed him. Listen to me or they will kill all of you."

Becker couldn't believe Joy's treachery. What was she hoping to gain? These guys didn't negotiate.

The Big B laughed. "What sadar? You're bluffing, there's just you two ugly women."

Joy, forever the performer, stuck her breasts in the goonda's face and shouted, "we're beautiful. We are pure. We will break free from the cycle of reincarnation long before you cocksuckers."

The goonda launched his spear. His followers gasped. Meena fell back, pinned to the floor, the Glock dropping to the cold marble and sliding out of her reach. Joy turned to her sister and started laughing manically. It was all over.

Becker and Ajinder stared at each other. What could they do? The game was up. The Big B pushed Joy roughly out of the way.

"Now we will see if you're a man or a woman. And then we'll kill you both. And the hostages will be decapitated in the morning. We would have liked to have made an example of the cop on the Maidan, but the palace steps will do just as well. Hindustan!"

His followers shouted in unison.

"Hindustan."

The Big B picked up the gun and shot Joy in the back. The bearded lady fell hard onto the marble and bled. The goonda fired bullet after bullet into the prone woman until the gun was empty. The Kali Yug men crowded in on Meena. Becker could no longer see her or the bound hostages.

Ajinder pushed him out of the way.

"We have to do something. I can't stand here watching them kill my brother. I can't."

Becker nodded. This is how it would end. Loyalty would kill him. He pulled the tickets and the keys from his jacket and slid them under a vase next to the ballroom's doorway. He nodded at Ajinder. They stepped into the room as one, a turbaned giant and a tired pensioner. Becker honed in on the gun. It was only a few meters away, lying forgotten. The Sadar had seen it too and raced for it. But he was slow and large and even in the gloom the Kali Yug gang spotted him immediately and ran towards him. It was Becker's moment. He pushed himself off the door frame and skidded across the wet marble. A second later the gun was in his hands. The Sikh roared, fending off a dozen men. Becker fumbled the magazine out of the Glock. He ripped the ammunition box open and squeezed the bullets into the magazine…one, two, three, four…he wasn't fast enough. The Big B loomed in front of him, the tip of his spear inches away from Becker's face.

"Bloody firangi," he spat in English. "India is for Indians."

He pulled back his arm. Everything slowed down. The harsh sounds of grunting ultra-violence softened. The spear retreated, then jetted towards him. This was the end. Becker sensed peace.

A bright flash crashed through Becker's vision and the speed and sound of the real world were back with a vengeance. The Big B stumbled backwards, a little too slowly as it turned out. Tagore flashed the dead guard's wooden pole at the chief goonda. Its end was on fire. The Big B howled when it connected with his chest a second time. Becker turned and pointed the gun at a wiry young man who was about to sink a chopper into Ajinder's chest. He pulled the trigger. The gun roared. The attacker fell, his arm almost torn off. Meena was nowhere to be seen. Becker steadied his hand and picked out another man. He pulled the trigger. He missed. He pulled the trigger again. The man's head exploded. The remaining dozen or so goondas ran into the night.

Tagore was sitting on the cold marble. He looked exhausted, and his beard was unruly. His club had burnt out. The Big B was gone. Ajinder untied his brother and Madhurima's husband. Becker was shaking.

"As-salāmu ʿalaykum. I am Emran, Madhu's husband. You are Becker."

He was a tall, gaunt man, but there was a good light in his eyes.

"Wa ʿalaykumu s-salām," Becker replied.

"You saved my life. Thanks."

"Not yet."

He flicked on his nekphone and connected to Madhu.

"Now. You need to leave now."

He flicked the phone off again.

"We have to move. I will take you to your wife."

He quickly and discreetly loaded the rest of the bullets into the Glock's magazine and slid to the doorway where he retrieved the tickets and the key. As he rose, Meena eyed him intensely.

"You have two tickets."

"Yes. But they're not for you. Tagore just saved your life. Joy is dead. Your brothers need you. You have to stay."

"Then who are they for, Becker?"

He liked her smile.

"I have an idea. Do you trust me?"

"Becker, you're a darling. You helped me get rid of my sister, you helped free Ajinder's brother. You're my hero, Becker. I trust you. I owe you. Idea away, babu."

Becker nodded and waved for the others.

"Friends, to finish my mission, I need to do one more thing. I need to deliver Emran to his wife. But the Big B and his thugs will be on our tails. They must know where we're going."

Tagore growled. "Where are we going?"

Becker turned to the dwarf. "The airport. Right now."

"How are we going?"

"We need a car, a big car for all of us. From here to the airport, the roads should be dry."

Ajinder, now carrying Vicky and Behan, Pavan, Meena, Tagore, Emran, and Becker — a Sikh hotel doorman and his brother, a showman family of low caste victims of a chemical spill, a former police commissioner and a Britisher — ran towards the palace's gates as one. An unlikely group of Kolkatans, Becker thought. The moon stood high in the sky. In the distance, they could hear shouting. Ajinder nodded down the street. "I know that noise. A mob is coming. They will torch this place. They have orders. We better get going the other direction. Otherwise they'll torch us as well."

They half walked and half ran. Becker was out of breath quickly. He wished he'd stayed in better shape for the apocalypse. But who was to have known? Meena sidled up to Becker.

"You still have the gun?"

Becker nodded.

"Give it to me. I'm a better shot than you."

"I did ok in there."

Meena flashed her best smile.

"You did. You saved us, Becker. But I actually quite enjoy killing bastards. I don't hesitate. As long as you're in Kolkata, you need someone to watch your back."

Becker hated shooting the gun. He handed it to Meena.

"Get us a car."

"You can drive?"

"Sure."

"Let's take this one then."

Meena smashed the driver's window of a parked-up yellow cab with the butt of the gun, opened the door, and pulled a bundle of wires from under the steering wheel. She ripped half of them from their sockets. Then she cracked open the steering lock and connected a couple of wires. The car's engine roared into life.

"I killed the self-drive. You drive, Becker."

She grinned at him seductively and moved onto the passenger seat.

"I'll be your point man/woman." Meena laughed shrilly. She

had the Glock in her right hand, presumably scanning the street for goondas.

Ajinder, Pavan, the Little Ones, and Emran piled in the back. Becker forced the car into gear and lurched off the curb.

———

Netaji Subhash Chandra Bose International Airport loomed out of the evening smog. The plane to Delhi was due to take off in an hour. The departure level was thronged by thousands of desperate souls.

"No point stopping here," Meena decided. "Round the back."

Becker plowed slowly through the crowd, persistently if not altogether aggressive. They came off the departure ramp and left the terminal area. To their left, a high fence separated them from the runways. Meena waved Becker towards the first gate. It was manned by a single javan. As they pulled up, Meena leaned out of her window and put the gun in the poor guy's face.

"Go home, it's all over. No one will ever pay you for sitting here."

He waved them through.

The two 797 Teslas stood in the same parking bays as they had done the week before. Becker stopped between the two huge aircraft. No one told them to leave. Whatever order there'd been three days earlier, it had almost evaporated. Several heavily armed soldiers stood around the single rickety boarding bridge that led to the front door of one of the planes. Tonight's taxi to Delhi.

"I'll park it. You sort out your life, Becker. Leave the Little Ones and Ajinder with me. I'll give a lift back into town to whoever doesn't make it onto that plane."

Becker looked at Meena. He wasn't quite sure what to do. He wasn't quite sure whether he should ask for the gun back. Meena grinned in the evening light.

"I'll keep the gun. Trust me, Becker. You can't take it on the flight."

"Thanks, Meena, you're a star."

She grinned and stuck her tongue out at him. He noticed that it had been pierced three times. He felt old. He felt an acute longing, but he wasn't sure for what. Not for Kolkata, that was for sure. Emran had stepped from the car. Becker followed. Meena took over the wheel and roared off, with the Little Ones waving in the rear window. The yellow Ambassador rattled off into the night. No long goodbyes. She could drive, even though auto-drive technology had been compulsory longer than she'd been an adult.

Madhu was waiting by the boarding bridge, clutching her handbag. Becker almost enjoyed the expressions that accumulated on her face when she saw them emerge out of the shadow of the plane.

"Oh my God."

She fell into her husband's arms. Becker looked away. Beyond the woman who'd been his remote guardian angel all his life, into the eyes of death. The Big B stepped out from behind the plane's huge front wheels. He carried a vicious looking crossbow, loaded with two arrows. Becker sensed Madhu's husband tensing up next to him. Emran must have seen him too. The goonda hadn't been spotted by the soldiers yet. But alerting them wouldn't stop him firing his weapon.

Becker stepped forward and inched in front of Madhu and her husband.

"I don't mind shooting you first, Britisher. I guess I should have listened to Joy. But I'm not stupid. I put it all together. Whatever ticket you have for that plane, it's mine. Let's go."

The Big B stepped out into the open, hiding his weapon behind his back. The soldiers looked at the man dressed only in a smutty gamcha doubtfully. But he also wore a Brahmin's thread, so they let him be. Becker pulled the two tickets out of his jacket, the goonda by his side. Out of the corner of his eye he could see

Madhu staring at him. She didn't look put out. He hadn't really failed her. The Big B pushed him up the boarding bridge. He could smell the man's sweat. He wouldn't sit next to this monster for the next three hours. He would push with all his might. Becker turned towards his captor as quick as he could. Not very quick at all. The Big B snarled a torrent of threats at him. Becker took another step towards the goonda. There was no stopping him. The boarding bridge shook. Becker grabbed the railing. The goonda slipped and was gone. Becker heard him scream, but he was gone. Confused, Becker turned.

The Big B lay trapped below him, his left leg broken and twisted. He had slid right through the gap between two steps. He was stuck half way up to the plane and he looked grotesque. The two soldiers were climbing towards them, two steps at a time, guns drawn. It was their job to keep access to the aircraft clear. Becker towered above them trying to look innocent. He didn't think he was doing a great job. The Big B, the Kali Yug goonda, raised his crossbow just as the first soldier reached him. Neither man hesitated. As the impact of the Big B's arrow threw the javan backwards, he shot the goonda in the stomach. The Big B roared in pain, but he couldn't move, his right leg was trapped, his left broken and twisted, his stomach now dripping onto the runway below the bridge. The javan pulled the arrow from his thick jacket and snapped it in half. He looked at his colleague for affirmation and shot the goonda again. Without further ceremony, the two men pulled the corpse off the boarding bridge and dumped him on the tarmac. Becker re-descended.

"This man had kidnapped you?"

Becker nodded.

"You will have to give a statement. We saved your life. You need to cover for us. We shot him in self-defense. He is Kali Yug. There will be consequences."

"When is the plane leaving?"

The two soldiers answered as one. "In twenty minutes. But you won't be on it. You can take the next one."

"I can't. I have tickets only for this one."

The javans laughed and kicked the goonda's corpse playfully.

"Then you'll have to stay in Kolkata, Britisher. We can't let you go. Otherwise we're in trouble. Our body cams don't work. And we're the last line of defense here. If we're pulled off this job, this airport will stop functioning. So, what do you want us to do?"

Becker grinned at them. "Arrest all the usual suspects."

He rejoined Madhu and Emran. They stood in shock and stared up at the airplane. A jeep pulled up out of the darkness. The pilot and a couple of crew members got out and raced up the bridge. The soldiers nodded at Becker.

"Looks like it's leaving now. But you're coming with us."

Becker turned to Madhu and handed her the two tickets.

"This is it, Madhu. When we parted twenty years ago, I always thought we would see each other again. This time, I am not sure. I think we've had our run."

She started crying. Emran, ashen-faced, took the tickets off her. He shook Becker's hand and started heading up the boarding bridge without another word. Madhu stood shaking.

"You have to go, Madhu. The plane will not wait. And Devi needs her mother. Please go."

"I will stay with you. Emran is safe. You kept your promise and more. I must repay you. We go to Darjeeling."

Becker shook his head.

"Don't waste the second ticket. You will miss him. And your daughter. What would India be without family? At least there will be an India somewhere else, even if this one here is swallowed by the sea."

"And you will drown with it?"

Becker shook his head.

"I don't intend to."

The yellow Ambassador emerged slowly between the two planes. Tagore sat on the roof, waving at no one in particular. Meena was at the wheel, leaning out towards Becker, clutching the Glock. He pulled the keys from his pocket.

"I will find your house, Madhu. I will take Meena and the Little Ones and Ajinder and his brother with me. We will be safe from the waters up there. And I will be surrounded by warriors.

Madhu swallowed hard.

"We were the best when the world was still functioning, Becker. That's why I could count on a Britisher helping a Hindu woman he loves save her Muslim husband. There's hope left in this world, Becker."

He nodded at her and waved, and she brushed her hand across his cheek, the only time she had explicitly and definitely touched him while looking into his eyes in forty years. Then she turned, shaking, and ascended. As if into the heavens. A second later the plane had swallowed her up and the door shut. The two javans pulled the boarding bridge away.

Meena stepped out of the Ambassador and strolled towards the soldiers.

"Defenders of our great nation, let this Britisher go."

"Or what?" one of the guards asked, looking hardly worried. How looks could be deceiving.

"Or I will shoot you both in the face."

The second javan laughed. Meena pulled her gun and shot him first. Then she shot his colleague. Then she collected their guns and ammunition while Tagore pulled their boots off. The plane started moving.

Becker, in severe shock, fumbled for the set of keys. Meena stepped over the two dead soldiers towards him.

"What else where you going to do?"

"I'm fucked now. I will never leave."

"You didn't want to leave, Becker. You were just looking for an excuse. What's with these keys?"

He threw them at her.

"Madhu's paradise home in the mountains near Darjeeling. Perfect for agricultural activities, I've been told. Large enough for a family."

Meena laughed and pulled her shirt up.

"You're going to get used to some real affection, Becker. You Britishers are all deviants, aren't you? And don't tell me you're too old. This could be the beginning of a new India."

Becker shook his head. He had nothing to say. The 797 Tesla was out on the runway now, in position. The engines started to roar, and the huge, bulky plane started moving. One by one the passenger windows slid past, but the plane was too far away to recognize anyone. There was one last thing to do. Becker pressed his nekphone into action and dialed Scotland.

"Hi Devi."

"Hi Becker, I just saw you sent the arrival time. I've got passage for two from London to Edinburgh. I see you soon. You're amazing."

He didn't have the courage to tell her the truth. He could barely admit it to himself.

"Madhu is looking forward to seeing you, Devi."

"Becker, you're the best."

He clicked off and turned to Meena.

"Tomorrow, we remove that thing from my neck."

She nodded and gave him her best coquettish smile.

"Me and the Little Ones will look after you. Ajinder will never leave your side. You will grow old with dignity, Becker, watching your vegetables grow and enjoying our sunsets with us."

She handed him the Glock.

"I'll drive. I rather like it."

───────

Retirement turned out to be the best thing Becker could do in a drowning world. He looked out over the Darjeeling hills. The fields below the house were ready to be harvested. Pavan's kids would start in the morning. Meena had just left his pot of afternoon tea by his side. Her smile still lingered in his mind as his gaze returned to the mountains. With the collapse of industry, the air in the Himalayas had cleared, and he could see, far in the distance, the summit of Everest. The Mount Kangchenjunga massif loomed right in front of him. He'd enjoyed the same view every day for the past fifteen years.

"Hey Becker, is that you?"

He saw a lithe shape coming up the trail by the house. His eyes had long been getting weaker. But that voice. He knew that voice from of a thousand, a million voices. He pushed himself up from his resting chair. He felt light. The sun felt soft on his old skin.

"Hey Madhu, is that you?"

He let himself fall into her arms.

Dear reader,

We hope you enjoyed reading Kolkata Noir. Please take a moment to leave a review, even if it's a short one. Your opinion is important to us.

Discover more books by Tom Vater at https://www.nextchapter.pub/authors/tom-vater

Want to know when one of our books is free or discounted? Join the newsletter at http://eepurl.com/bqqB3H

Best regards,

Tom Vater and the Next Chapter Team

ACKNOWLEDGMENTS

During the Raj, Calcutta was the world's second most economically powerful metropolis. In 2019, Kolkata, eastern India's largest city, stands at a crossroads. Unlike Delhi and Mumbai, the West Bengal Capital is anything but an economic powerhouse. Its remote eastern location and decades of communist rule have seen to this. Many young middle-class Bengalis are leaving for other cities or go abroad for lack of opportunity back home. But this stasis has also kept crime rates and pollution levels lower than in other Indian cities. It has kept American fast food out of the inner city. The sheer amount of remarkable British and Bengali architecture surviving from the early 20th century is incredible. The communal tensions between Hindus and Muslims are surely present, but have not burst into the open with the same ferocious violence as in parts of northern and central India.

For foreign visitors, Kolkata is a challenging but rewarding time travel experience. Kolkatans are extraordinarily friendly. There are book shops. The food is excellent. One can walk. It's pretty safe. Kolkata, bustling, hustling, almost on its knees one day and flying high without a license the next, is never ever boring.

Most of Kolkata Noir was written in Kolkata.

In 2019, I was selected by the Goethe Institut/Max Müller Bhavan Kolkata to write crime fiction set in the West Bengal capital as part of the annual Indo-European Artist Residency. Once in the West Bengal capital, Director Friso Maecker and

Program Officer Sharmistha Sarker were staunch supporters of my ideas and our discussions helped form this small contribution to the rich cultural tapestry of the city.

For eight weeks I shared a historic house in Ballygunge with three other artists participating in the residency — Sophie Cousinié from France, Imogen Butler-Cole from the UK, and Aditi Aggarwal from Delhi — under the watchful eye of inimitable house manager Nandu. We set out to create a theatre play, illustrations, paintings, photographs, and fiction. I am very grateful to the other artists for their company, support, insights, and ideas.

The residency culminated in a group exhibition at Experimenter Gallery, where I exhibited a series of images entitled 'Destroy Everything Beautiful', a nod to the rapid changes the city is undergoing. I read a Kolkata-based short story while being tattooed — the word 'Noir' — by fellow writer Laure Siegel — to an audience transfixed by the spectacle as much as by my prose.

Special thanks to writer Aurko Maitra who graciously invited me to tag along during his nightly meanderings through many of the city's lesser-known and marginal districts, particularly Dhapa, Tangra, and Topsia. Aurko and his friend SK Shaquib, who was just as generous with his time and thoughts, introduced me to countless Kolkata luminaries — hitmen, movie directors, cage fighters, artists, and gangsters. Park Circus nights…!

I'd also like to thank Chiru Sur, Devi Ganguly, Gaurav Pandey, and Joyana Medhi.

Huge thanks to Laure Siegel for pointing out (life's) incongruities, plot holes, and continuity issues, in the text and beyond. To PR manager Chris Roy for promoting my books around the world. And to Hans Kemp, my former Crime Wave Press partner. Finally, thanks to careful reader Manis Ender for spotting several text errors. And much appreciation to writer James Newman who decided to drop by late one night.

I am indebted to Kolkata's famous detective Feluda, the brain child of legendary Bengali film maker Satayjit Ray, who provided the initial spark for Kolkata Noir. I made no attempt to revive or copy Ray's story-telling, and yet Kolkata Noir might never have been written had it not been for my long love affair with the city of which Feluda is such an integral part.

Kolkata Noir, a crime fiction cycle of three novellas, is set in the past, the present, and the future.

The first story — Calcutta — takes place in 1999. The plot is in part an homage to the classic French Noir movie Les Diaboliques.

The second story — Kolkata — takes place in 2019. The plot is in part an homage to Sonar Kella, one of West Bengal's best-known crime stories, written by well-known art house film maker Satyajit Ray.

The third story — Killkata — takes place in 2039, when the city is half submerged thanks to rising sea levels. The plot is in part an homage to the 1942 movie Casablanca.

ABOUT THE AUTHOR

Tom Vater is an Asia-based writer.

He has published some 20 books – novels, nonfiction, illustrated books and guidebooks, all on Asian subjects.

Tom has written four crime fiction novels. The Devil's Road to Kathmandu - the third English language edition is out with Next Chapter - is a travel thriller set on the 70s hippie trail between London and Kathmandu. A Spanish translation is out with ExploraEditorial.

The Detective Maier trilogy - The Cambodian Book of the Dead, The Man with the Golden Mind and The Monsoon Ghost Image, a Southeast Asia based series of crime novels that follows the exploits of a former conflict journalist turned private eye.

Tom writes for many publications, including The Guardian, The Times, The Wall Street Journal, The Daily Telegraph, and the Nikkei Asian Review. He co-authored the bestselling Sacred Skin – Thailand's Spirit Tattoos (2011). He is also co-author of several documentary screenplays, including The Most Secret Place on Earth (2008), a feature on the CIA's covert war in Laos in the 60s and 70s.

Tom is on Twitter, Facebook and LinkedIn.
www.tomvater.com
https://www.clippings.me/users/tomvater
Twitter: @tomvater
Instagram: https://www.instagram.com/tomvaterwrites/
Facebook: https://www.facebook.com/tomvater

Kolkata Noir
ISBN: 978-4-86751-636-2

Published by
Next Chapter
2-5-6 SANNO
SANNO BRIDGE
143-0023 Ota-Ku, Tokyo
+818035793528

31st May 2022